Boyhood in Norway

Hjalmar Hjorth Boyesen

BOYHOOD IN NORWAY

STORIES OF BOY-LIFE IN THE LAND OF THE MIDNIGHT SUN

BY

HJALMAR HJORTH BOYESEN

CONTENTS

THE BATTLE OF THE RAFTS

I. THE ORIGIN OF THE WAR

A deadly feud was raging among the boys of Numedale. The East-Siders hated the West-Siders, and thrashed them when they got a chance; and the West-Siders, when fortune favored them, returned the compliment with interest. It required considerable courage for a boy to venture, unattended by comrades, into the territory of the enemy; and no one took the risk unless dire necessity compelled him.

The hostile parties had played at war so long that they had forgotten that it was play; and now were actually inspired with the emotions which they had formerly simulated. Under the leadership of their chieftains, Halvor Reitan and Viggo Hook, they held councils of war, sent out scouts, planned midnight surprises, and fought at times mimic battles. I say mimic battles, because no one was ever killed; but broken heads and bruised limbs many a one carried home from these engagements, and unhappily one boy, named Peer Oestmo, had an eye put out by an arrow.

It was a great consolation to him that he became a hero to all the West-Siders and was promoted for bravery in the field to the rank of first lieutenant. He had the sympathy of all his companions in arms and got innumerable bites of apples, cancelled postage stamps, and colored advertising-labels in token of their esteem.

But the principal effect of this first serious wound was to invest the war with a breathless and all-absorbing interest. It was now no longer "make believe, " but deadly earnest. Blood had flowed; insults had been exchanged in due order, and offended honor cried for vengeance.

It was fortunate that the river divided the West-Siders from the East-Siders, or it would have been difficult to tell what might have happened. Viggo Hook, the West-Side general, was a handsome, high-spirited lad of fifteen, who was the last person to pocket an injury, as long as red blood flowed in his veins, as he was wont to express it. He was the eldest son of Colonel Hook of the regular army, and meant some day to be a Von Moltke or a Napoleon. He felt in his heart that he was destined for something great; and in conformity with this conviction assumed a superb behavior, which his comrades found very admirable.

He had the gift of leadership in a marked degree, and established his authority by a due mixture of kindness and severity. Those boys whom he honored with his confidence were absolutely attached to him. Those whom, with magnificent arbitrariness, he punished and persecuted, felt meekly that they had probably deserved it; and if they had not, it was somehow in the game.

There never was a more absolute king than Viggo, nor one more abjectly courted and admired. And the amusing part of it was that he was at heart a generous and good-natured lad, but possessed with a lofty ideal of heroism, which required above all things that whatever he said or did must be striking. He dramatized, as it were, every phrase he uttered and every act he performed, and modelled himself alternately after Napoleon and Wellington, as he had seen them represented in the old engravings which decorated the walls in his father's study.

He had read much about heroes of war, ancient and modern, and he lived about half his own life imagining himself by turns all sorts of grand characters from history or fiction.

His costume was usually in keeping with his own conception of these characters, in so far as his scanty opportunities permitted. An old, broken sword of his father's, which had been polished until it "flashed" properly, was girded to a brass- mounted belt about his waist; an ancient, gold-braided, military cap, which was much too large, covered his curly head; and four tarnished brass buttons, displaying the Golden Lion of Norway, gave a martial air to his blue jacket, although the rest were plain horn.

But quite independently of his poor trappings Viggo was to his comrades an august personage. I doubt if the Grand Vizier feels more flattered and gratified by the favor of the Sultan than little Marcus Henning did, when Viggo condescended to be civil to him.

Marcus was small, round-shouldered, spindle-shanked, and freckle-faced. His hair was coarse, straight, and the color of maple sirup; his nose was broad and a little flattened at the point, and his clothes had a knack of never fitting him. They were made to grow in and somehow he never caught up with them, he once said, with no intention of being funny. His father, who was Colonel Hook's nearest neighbor, kept a modest country shop, in which you could buy anything, from dry goods and groceries to shoes and medicines. You would have to be very ingenious to ask for a thing which Henning could not supply. The smell in the store carried out the same idea; for it was a mixture of all imaginable smells under the sun.

Now, it was the chief misery of Marcus that, sleeping, as he did, in the room behind the store, he had become so impregnated with this curious composite smell that it followed him like an odoriferous halo, and procured him a number of unpleasant nicknames. The principal ingredient was salted herring; but there was also a suspicion of tarred ropes, plug tobacco, prunes, dried codfish, and oiled tarpaulin.

It was not so much kindness of heart as respect for his own dignity which made Viggo refrain from calling Marcus a "Muskrat" or a "Smelling-Bottle. " And yet Marcus regarded this gracious forbearance on his part as the mark of a noble soul. He had been compelled to accept these offensive nicknames, and, finding rebellion vain, he had finally acquiesced in them.

He never loved to be called a "Muskrat, " though he answered to the name mechanically. But when Viggo addressed him as "base minion," in his wrath, or as "Sergeant Henning, " in his sunnier moods, Marcus felt equally complimented by both terms, and vowed in his grateful soul eternal allegiance and loyalty to his chief.

He bore kicks and cuffs with the same admirable equanimity; never complained when he was thrown into a dungeon in a deserted pigsty for breaches of discipline of which he was entirely guiltless, and trudged uncomplainingly through rain and sleet and snow, as scout or spy, or what-not, at the behest of his exacting commander.

It was all so very real to him that he never would have thought of doubting the importance of his mission. He was rather honored by the trust reposed in him, and was only intent upon earning a look or word of scant approval from the superb personage whom he worshipped.

Halvor Reitan, the chief of the East-Siders, was a big, burly peasant lad, with a pimpled face, fierce blue eyes, and a shock of towy hair. But he had muscles as hard as twisted ropes, and sinews like steel.

He had the reputation, of which he was very proud, of being the strongest boy in the valley, and though he was scarcely sixteen years old, he boasted that he could whip many a one of twice his years. He had, in fact, been so praised for his strength that he never neglected to accept, or even to create, opportunities for displaying it.

His manner was that of a bully; but it was vanity and not malice which made him always spoil for a fight. He and Viggo Hook had attended the parson's "Confirmation Class, " together, and it was there their hostility had commenced.

Halvor, who conceived a dislike of the tall, rather dainty, and disdainful Viggo, with his aquiline nose and clear, aristocratic features, determined, as he expressed it, to take him down a peg or two; and the more his challenges were ignored the more persistent he grew in his insults.

He dubbed Viggo "Missy. " He ran against him with such violence in the hall that he knocked his head against the wainscoting; he tripped him up on the stairs by means of canes and sticks; and he hired his partisans who sat behind Viggo to stick pins into him, while he recited his lessons. And when all these provocations proved unavailing he determined to dispense with any pretext, but simply thrash his enemy within an inch of his life at the first opportunity which presented itself. He grew to hate Viggo and was always aching to molest him.

Halvor saw plainly enough that Viggo despised him, and refused to notice his challenges, not so much because he was afraid of him, as because he regarded himself as a superior being who could afford to ignore insults from an inferior, without loss of dignity.

During recess the so-called "genteel boys, " who had better clothes and better manners than the peasant lads, separated themselves from the rest, and conversed or played with each other. No one will wonder that such behavior was exasperating to the poorer boys. I am far from defending Viggo's behavior in this instance. He was here, as everywhere, the acknowledged leader; and therefore more cordially hated than the rest. It was the Roundhead hating the Cavalier; and the Cavalier making merry at the expense of the Roundhead.

There was only one boy in the Confirmation Class who was doubtful as to what camp should claim him, and that was little Marcus Henning. He was a kind of amphibious animal who, as he thought, really belonged nowhere. His father was of peasant origin, but by his prosperity and his occupation had risen out of the class to which he was formerly attached, without yet rising into the ranks of the gentry, who now, as always, looked with scorn upon interlopers. Thus it came to pass that little Marcus, whose inclinations drew him toward Viggo's party, was yet forced to associate with the partisans of Halvor Reitan.

It was not a vulgar ambition "to pretend to be better than he was" which inspired Marcus with a desire to change his allegiance, but a deep, unreasoning admiration for Viggo Hook. He had never seen any one who united so many superb qualities, nor one who looked every inch as noble as he did.

It did not discourage him in the least that his first approaches met with no cordial reception. His offer to communicate to Viggo where there was a hawk's nest was coolly declined, and even the attractions of fox dens and rabbits' burrows were valiantly resisted. Better luck he had with a pair of fan-tail pigeons, his most precious treasure, which Viggo rather loftily consented to accept, for, like most genteel boys in the valley, he was an ardent pigeon-fancier, and had long vainly importuned his father to procure him some of the rarer breeds

He condescended to acknowledge Marcus's greeting after that, and to respond to his diffident "Good-morning" and "Good-evening, " and Marcus was duly grateful for such favors. He continued to woo his idol with raisins and ginger-snaps from the store, and other delicate attentions, and bore the snubs which often fell to his lot with humility and patience.

But an event soon occurred which was destined to change the relations of the two boys. Halvor Reitan called a secret meeting of his partisans, among whom he made the mistake to include Marcus, and agreed with them to lie in ambush at the bend of the road, where it entered the forest, and attack Viggo Hook and his followers. Then, he observed, he would "make him dance a jig that would take the starch out of him. "

The others declared that this would be capital fun, and enthusiastically promised their assistance. Each one selected his particular antipathy to thrash, though all showed a marked preference for Viggo, whom, however, for reason of politeness, they were obliged to leave to the chief. Only one boy sat silent, and made no offer to thrash anybody, and that was Marcus Henning.

"Well, Muskrat, " cried Halvor Reitan, "whom are you going to take on your conscience? "

"No one, " said Marcus.

"Put the Muskrat in your pocket, Halvor, " suggested one of the boys; "he is so small, and he has got such a hard bullet head, you might use him as a club. "

"Well, one thing is sure, " shouted Halvor, as a dark suspicion shot through his brain, "if you don't keep mum, you will be a mighty sick coon the day after to-morrow. "

Marcus made no reply, but got up quietly, pulled a rubber sling from his pocket, and began, with the most indifferent manner in the world, to shoot stones down the river. He managed during this exercise, which everybody found perfectly natural, to get out of the crowd, and, without seeming to have any purpose whatever, he continued to put a couple of hundred yards between himself and his companion.

"Look a-here, Muskrat, " he heard Halvor cry, "you promised to keep mum. "

Marcus, instead of answering, took to his heels and ran.

"Boys, the scoundrel is going to betray us! " screamed the chief. "Now come, boys! We've got to catch him, dead or alive. "

A volley of stones, big and little, was hurled after the fugitive, who now realizing his position ran for dear life. The stones hailed down round about him; occasionally one vicious missile would whiz past his ear, and send a cold shudder through him. The tramp of his pursuers sounded nearer and nearer, and his one chance of escape was to throw himself into the only boat, which he saw on this side of the river, and push out into the stream before he was overtaken.

He had his doubts as to whether he could accomplish this, for the blood rushed and roared in his ears, the hill-side billowed under his feet, and it seemed as if the trees were all running a race in the opposite direction, in order to betray him to his enemies.

A stone gave him a thump in the back, but though he felt a gradual heat spreading from the spot which it hit, he was conscious of no pain.

Presently a larger missile struck him in the neck, and he heard a breathless snorting close behind him. That was the end; he gave himself up for lost, for those boys would have no mercy on him if they captured him.

But in the next moment he heard a fall and an oath, and the voice was that of Halvor Reitan. He breathed a little more freely as he saw the river run with its swelling current at his feet. Quite mechanically, without clearly knowing what he did, he sprang into the boat, grabbed a boat-hook, and with three strong strokes pushed himself out into the deep water.

At that instant a dozen of his pursuers reached the river bank, and he saw dimly their angry faces and threatening gestures, and heard the stones drop into the stream about him. Fortunately the river was partly dammed, in order to accumulate water for the many saw-mills under the falls. It would therefore have been no very difficult feat to paddle across, if his aching arms had had an atom of strength left in them. As soon as he was beyond the reach of flying stones he seated himself in the stern, took an oar, and after having bathed his throbbing forehead in the cold water, managed, in fifteen minutes, to make the further bank. Then he dragged himself wearily up the hill-side to Colonel Hook's mansion, and when he had given his message to Viggo, fell into a dead faint.

How could Viggo help being touched by such devotion? He had seen the race through a fieldglass from his pigeon-cot, but had been unable to make out its meaning, nor had he remotely dreamed that he was himself the cause of the cruel chase. He called his mother, who soon perceived that Marcus's coat was saturated with blood in the back, and undressing him, she found that a stone, hurled by a sling, had struck him, slid a few inches along the rib, and had lodged in the fleshy part of his left side.

A doctor was now sent for; the stone was cut out without difficulty, and Marcus was invited to remain as Viggo's guest until he recovered. He felt so honored by this invitation that he secretly prayed he might remain ill for a month; but the wound showed an abominable readiness to heal, and before three days were past Marcus could not feign any ailment which his face and eye did not belie.

He then, with a heavy heart, betook himself homeward, and installed himself once more among his accustomed smells behind the store, and pondered sadly on the caprice of the fate which had made Viggo a high-nosed, handsome gentleman, and him—Marcus Henning—an under-grown, homely, and unrefined drudge. But in spite of his failure to answer this question, there was joy within him at the thought that he had saved this handsome face of Viggo's from disfigurement, and—who could know? —perhaps would earn a claim upon his gratitude.

It was this series of incidents which led to the war between the East-Siders and the West-Siders. It was a mere accident that the partisans of Viggo Hook lived on the west side of the river, and those of Halvor Reitan mostly on the east side.

Viggo, who had a chivalrous sense of fair play, would never have molested any one without good cause; but now his own safety, and, as he persuaded himself, even his life, was in danger, and he had no choice but to take measures in self-defence. He surrounded himself with a trusty body-guard, which attended him wherever he went. He sent little Marcus, in whom he recognized his most devoted follower, as scout into the enemy's territory, and swelled his importance enormously by lending him his field-glass to assist him in his perilous observations.

Occasionally an unhappy East-Sider was captured on the west bank of the river, court-martialed, and, with much solemnity, sentenced to death as a spy, but paroled for an indefinite period, until it should suit his judges to execute the sentence. The East-Siders, when they captured a West-Sider, went to work with less ceremony; they simply thrashed their captive soundly and let him run, if run he could.

Thus months passed. The parson's Confirmation Class ceased, and both the opposing chieftains were confirmed on the same day; but

Viggo stood at the head of the candidates, while Halvor had his place at the bottom. [1]

[1] In Norway confirmation is always preceded by a public examination of the candidates in the aisle of the church. The order in which they are arranged is supposed to indicate their attainments, but does, as a rule, indicate the rank and social position of their parents.

During the following winter the war was prosecuted with much zeal, and the West-Siders, in imitation of Robin Hood and his Merry Men, armed themselves with cross-bows, and lay in ambush in the underbrush, aiming their swift arrows against any intruder who ventured to cross the river.

Nearly all the boys in the valley between twelve and sixteen became enlisted on the one side or the other, and there were councils of war, marches, and counter-marches without number, occasional skirmishes, but no decisive engagements. Peer Oestmo, to be sure, had his eye put out by an arrow, as has already been related, for the East-Siders were not slow to imitate the example of their enemies, in becoming expert archers.

Marcus Henning was captured by a hostile outpost, and was being conducted to the abode of the chief, when, by a clever stratagem, he succeeded in making his escape.

The East-Siders despatched, under a flag of truce, a most insulting caricature of General Viggo, representing him as a rooster that seemed on the point of bursting with an excess of dignity.

These were the chief incidents of the winter, though there were many others of less consequence that served to keep the boys in a delightful state of excitement. They enjoyed the war keenly, though they pretended to themselves that they were being ill-used and suffered terrible hardships. They grumbled at their duties, brought complaints against their officers to the general, and did, in fact, all the things that real soldiers would have been likely to do under similar circumstances.

II.

THE CLASH OF ARMS

When the spring is late in Norway, and the heat comes with a sudden rush, the mountain streams plunge with a tremendous noise down into the valleys, and the air is filled far and near with the boom and roar of rushing waters. The glaciers groan, and send their milk-white torrents down toward the ocean. The snow-patches in the forest glens look gray and soiled, and the pines perspire a delicious resinous odor which cheers the soul with the conviction that spring has come.

But the peasant looks anxiously at the sun and the river at such times, for he knows that there is danger of inundation. The lumber, which the spring floods set afloat in enormous quantities, is carried by the rivers to the cities by the sea; there it is sorted according to the mark it bears, showing the proprietor, and exported to foreign countries.

In order to prevent log-jams, which are often attended with terrible disasters, men are stationed night and day at the narrows of the rivers. The boys, to whom all excitement is welcome, are apt to congregate in large numbers at such places, assisting or annoying the watchers, riding on the logs, or teasing the girls who stand up on the hillside, admiring the daring feats of the lumbermen.

It was on such a spring day, when the air was pungent with the smell of sprouting birch and pine, that General Viggo and his trusty army had betaken themselves to the cataract to share in the sport. They were armed with their bows, as usual, knowing that they were always liable to be surprised by their vigilant enemy. Nor were they in this instance disappointed, for Halvor Reitan, with fifty or sixty followers, was presently visible on the east side, and it was a foregone conclusion that if they met there would be a battle.

The river, to be sure, separated them, but the logs were at times so densely packed that it was possible for a daring lad to run far out into the river, shoot his arrow and return to shore, leaping from log to log. The Reitan party was the first to begin this sport, and an arrow hit General Viggo's hat before he gave orders to repel the assault.

Cool and dignified as he was, he could not consent to skip and jump on the slippery logs, particularly as he had no experience in this difficult exercise, while the enemy apparently had much. Paying no heed to the jeers of the lumbermen, who supposed he was afraid, he drew his troops up in line and addressed them as follows:

"Soldiers: You have on many previous occasions given me proof of your fidelity to duty and your brave and fearless spirit. I know that I can, now as always, trust you to shed glory upon our arms, and to maintain our noble fame and honorable traditions.

"The enemy is before us. You have heard and seen his challenge. It behooves us to respond gallantly. To jump and skip like rabbits is unmilitary and unsoldierlike. I propose that each of us shall select two large logs, tie them together, procure, if possible, a boat-hook or an oar, and, sitting astride the logs, boldly push out into the river. If we can advance in a tolerably even line, which I think quite possible, we can send so deadly a charge into the ranks of our adversaries that they will be compelled to flee. Then we will land on the east side, occupy the heights, and rout our foe.

"Now let each man do his duty. Forward, march! "

The lumbermen, whose sympathies were with the East-Siders, found this performance highly diverting, but Viggo allowed himself in nowise to be disturbed by their laughter or jeers. He marched his troops down to the river-front, commanded "Rest arms! " and repeated once more his instructions; then, flinging off his coat and waistcoat, he seized a boat-hook and ran some hundred yards along the bank of the stream.

The river-bed was here expanded to a wide basin, in which the logs floated lazily down to the cataract below. Trees and underbrush, which usually stood on dry land, were half-submerged in the yellow water, and the current gurgled slowly about their trunks with muddy foam and bubbles. Now and then a heap of lumber would get wedged in between the jutting rocks above the waterfall, and then the current slackened, only to be suddenly accelerated, when the exertions of the men had again removed the obstruction.

It was an exciting spectacle to see these daring fellows leap from log to log, with birch-bark shoes on their feet. They would ride on a heap of lumber down to the very edge of the cataract, dexterously jump off at the critical moment, and after half a dozen narrow escapes, reach the shore, only to repeat the dangerous experiment, as soon as the next opportunity offered itself.

It was the example of these hardy and agile lumbermen, trained from childhood to sport with danger, which inspired Viggo and his followers with a desire to show their mettle.

"Sergeant Henning, " said the General to his ever-faithful shadow, "take a squad of five men with you, and cut steering-poles for those for whom boat-hooks cannot be procured. You will be the last to leave shore. Report to me if any one fails to obey orders. "

"Shall be done, General, " Marcus responded, with a deferential military salute.

"The bows, you understand, will be slung by the straps across the backs of the men, while they steer and push with their poles. "

"Certainly, General, " said Marcus, with another salute.

"You may go. "

"All right, General, " answered Marcus, with a third salute.

And now began the battle. The East-Siders, fearing that a stratagem was intended, when they saw the enemy moving up the stream, made haste to follow their example, capturing on their way every stray log that came along. They sent ineffectual showers of arrows into the water, while the brave General Viggo, striding two big logs which he had tied together with a piece of rope, and with a boat-hook in his hand, pushed proudly at the head of his army into the middle of the wide basin.

Halvor Reitan was clever enough to see what it meant, and he was not going to allow the West-Siders to gain the heights above him, and attack him in the rear. He meant to prevent the enemy from landing, or, still better, he would meet him half-way, and drive him back to his own shore.

The latter, though not the wiser course, was the plan which Halvor Reitan adopted. To have a tussle with the high-nosed Viggo in the middle of the basin, to dislodge him from his raft—that seemed to

Halvor a delightful project. He knew that Viggo was a good swimmer, so he feared no dangerous consequences; and even if he had, it would not have restrained him. He was so much stronger than Viggo, and here was his much-longed-for opportunity.

With great despatch he made himself a raft of two logs, and seating himself astride them, with his legs in the water, put off from shore. He shouted to his men to follow him, and they needed no urging. Viggo was now near the middle of the basin, with twenty or thirty picked archers close behind him. They fired volley after volley of arrows against the enemy, and twice drove him back to the shore.

But Halvor Reitan, shielding his face with a piece of bark which he had picked up, pushed forward in spite of their onslaught, though one arrow knocked off his red-peaked cap, and another scratched his ear. Now he was but a dozen feet from his foe. He cared little for his bow now; the boat-hook was a far more effectual weapon.

Viggo saw at a glance that he meant to pull his raft toward him, and, relying upon his greater strength, fling him into the water.

His first plan would therefore be to fence with his own boat-hook, so as to keep his antagonist at a distance.

When Halvor made the first lunge at the nose of his raft, he foiled the attempt with his own weapon, and managed dexterously to give the hostile raft a downward push, which increased the distance between them.

"Take care, General! " said a respectful voice close to Viggo's ear. "There is a small log jam down below, which is getting bigger every moment. When it is got afloat, it will be dangerous out here. "

"What are you doing here, Sergeant? " asked the General, severely. "Did I not tell you to be the last to leave the shore? "

"You did, General, " Marcus replied, meekly, "and I obeyed. But I have pushed to the front so as to be near you. "

"I don't need you, Sergeant, " Viggo responded, "you may go to the rear. "

The booming of the cataract nearly drowned his voice and Marcus pretended not to hear it. A huge lumber mass was piling itself up among the rocks jutting out of the rapids, and a dozen men hanging like flies on the logs, sprang up and down with axes in their hands. They cut one log here and another there; shouted commands; and fell into the river amid the derisive jeers of the spectators; they scrambled out again and, dripping wet, set to work once more with a cheerful heart, to the mighty music of the cataract, whose thundering rhythm trembled and throbbed in the air.

The boys who were steering their rafts against each other in the comparatively placid basin were too absorbed in their mimic battle to heed what was going on below. Halvor and Viggo were fighting desperately with their boat-hooks, the one attacking and the other defending himself with great dexterity. They scarcely perceived, in their excitement, that the current was dragging them slowly toward the cataract; nor did they note the warning cries of the men and women on the banks.

Viggo's blood was hot, his temples throbbed, his eyes flashed. He would show this miserable clown who had dared to insult him, that the trained skill of a gentleman is worth more than the rude strength of a bully. With beautiful precision he foiled every attack; struck Halvor's boat-hook up and down, so that the water splashed about him, manoeuvring at the same time his own raft with admirable adroitness.

Cheer upon cheer rent the air, after each of his successful sallies, and his comrades, selecting their antagonists from among the enemy, now pressed forward, all eager to bear their part in the fray.

Splash! splash! splash! one East-Sider was dismounted, got an involuntary bath, but scrambled up on his raft again. The next time it was a West-Sider who got a ducking, but seemed none the worse for it. There was a yelling and a cheering, now from one side and now from the other, which made everyone forget that something was going on at that moment of greater importance than the mimic warfare of boys.

All the interest of the contending parties was concentrated on the duel of their chieftains. It seemed now really that Halvor was getting the worst of it. He could not get close enough to use his brawny muscles; and in precision of aim and adroitness of movement he was not Viggo's match.

Again and again he thrust his long-handled boat-hook angrily against the bottom (for the flooded parts of the banks were very shallow), to push the raft forward, but every time Viggo managed to turn it sideward, and Halvor had to exert all his presence of mind to keep his seat. Wild with rage he sprang up on his slender raft and made a vicious lunge at his opponent, who warded the blow with such force that the handle of the boat-hook broke, and Halvor lost his balance and fell into the water.

At this same instant a tremendous crash was heard from below, followed by a long rumble as of mighty artillery. A scream of horror went up from the banks, as the great lumber mass rolled down into the cataract, making a sudden suction which it seemed impossible that the unhappy boys could resist.

The majority of both sides, seeing their danger, beat, by means of their boat-hooks, a hasty retreat, and as they were in shallow water were hauled ashore by the lumbermen, who sprang into the river to save them.

When the clouds of spray had cleared away, only three figures were visible. Viggo, still astride of his raft, was fighting, not for his own life, but for that of his enemy, Halvor, who was struggling helplessly in the white rapids. Close behind his commander stood little Marcus on his raft, holding on, with one hand to the boat-hook which he had hewn, with all his might, into Viggo's raft, and with the other grasping the branch of a half-submerged tree.

"Save yourself, General! " he yelled, wildly. "Let go there. I can't hold on much longer. "

But Viggo did not heed. He saw nothing but the pale, frightened face of his antagonist, who might lose his life. With a desperate effort he flung his boat-hook toward him and succeeded this time in laying hold of the leather girdle about his waist. One hundred feet below yawned the foaming, weltering abyss, from which the white smoke ascended. If Marcus lost his grip, if the branch snapped no human power could save them; they were all dead men.

15

By this time the people on the shore had discovered that three lives were hanging on the brink of eternity. Twenty men had waded waist-deep into the current and had flung a stout rope to the noble little fellow who was risking his own life for his friend.

"Keep your hold, my brave lad! " they cried; "hold on another minute! "

"Grab the rope! " screamed others.

Marcus clinched his teeth, and his numb arms trembled, mist gathered in his eyes—his heart stood still. But with a clutch that seemed superhuman he held on. He had but one thought— Viggo, his chief! Viggo, his idol! Viggo, his general! He must save him or die with him. One end of the rope was hanging on the branch and was within easy reach; but he did not venture to seize it, lest the wrench caused by his motion might detach his hold on Viggo's raft.

Viggo, who just now was pulling Halvor out of the water, saw in an instant that he had by adding his weight to the raft, increased the chance of both being carried to their death. With quick resolution he plunged the beak of his own boat-hook into Marcus's raft, and shouted to Halvor to save himself. The latter, taking in the situation at a glance, laid hold of the handle of the boat-hook and together they pulled up alongside of Marcus and leaped aboard his raft, whereupon Viggo's raft drifted downward and vanished in a flash in the yellow torrent.

At that very instant Marcus's strength gave out; he relaxed his grip on the branch, which slid out of his hand, and they would inevitably have darted over the brink of the cataract if Viggo had not, with great adroitness, snatched the rope from the branch of the half-submerged tree.

A wild shout, half a cheer, half a cry of relief, went up from the banks, as the raft with the three lads was slowly hauled toward the shore by the lumbermen who had thrown the rope.

Halvor Reitan was the first to step ashore. But no joyous welcome greeted him from those whose sympathies had, a little while ago, been all on his side. He hung around uneasily for some minutes, feeling perhaps that he ought to say something to Viggo who had saved his life, but as he could not think of anything which did not seem foolish, he skulked away unnoticed toward the edge of the forest.

But when Viggo stepped ashore, carrying the unconscious Marcus in his arms, how the crowd rushed forward to gaze at him, to press his hands, to call down God's blessing upon him! He had never imagined that he was such a hero. It was Marcus, not he, to whom their ovation was due. But poor Marcus—it was well for him that he had fainted from over-exertion; for otherwise he would have fainted from embarrassment at the honors which would have been showered upon him.

The West-Siders, marching two abreast, with their bows slung across their shoulders, escorted their general home, cheering and shouting as they went. When they were half-way up the hillside, Marcus opened his eyes, and finding himself so close to his beloved general, blushed crimson, scarlet, and purple, and all the other shades that an embarrassed blush is capable of assuming.

"Please, General, " he stammered, "don't bother about me. "

Viggo had thought of making a speech exalting the heroism of his faithful follower. But he saw at a glance that his praise would be more grateful to Marcus, if he received it in private.

When, however, the boys gave him a parting cheer, in front of his father's mansion, he forgot his resolution, leaped up on the steps, and lifting the blushing Marcus above his head; called out:

"Three cheers for the bravest boy in Norway! "

BICEPS GRIMLUND'S CHRISTMAS VACATION

I.

The great question which Albert Grimlund was debating was fraught with unpleasant possibilities. He could not go home for the Christmas vacation, for his father lived in Drontheim, which is so far away from Christiania that it was scarcely worth while making the journey for a mere two-weeks' holiday. Then, on the other hand, he had an old great-aunt who lived but a few miles from the city. She had, from conscientious motives, he feared, sent him an invitation to pass Christmas with her. But Albert had a poor opinion of Aunt Elsbeth. He thought her a very tedious person. She had a dozen cats, talked of nothing but sermons and lessons, and asked him occasionally, with pleasant humor, whether he got many whippings at school. She failed to comprehend that a boy could not amuse himself forever by looking at the pictures in the old family Bible, holding yarn, and listening to oft-repeated stories, which he knew by heart, concerning the doings and sayings of his grandfather. Aunt Elsbeth, after a previous experience with her nephew, had come to regard boys as rather a reprehensible kind of animal, who differed in many of their ways from girls, and altogether to the boys' disadvantage.

Now, the prospect of being "caged" for two weeks with this estimable lady was, as I said, not at all pleasant to Albert. He was sixteen years old, loved out-door sports, and had no taste for cats. His chief pride was his muscle, and no boy ever made his acquaintance without being invited to feel the size and hardness of his biceps. This was a standing joke in the Latin school, and Albert was generally known among his companions as "Biceps" Grimlund. He was not very tall for his age, but broad-shouldered and deep-chested, with something in his glance, his gait, and his manners which showed that he had been born and bred near the sea. He cultivated a weather-beaten complexion, and was particularly proud when the skin "peeled" on his nose, which it usually did in the summer-time, during his visits to his home in the extreme north. Like most blond people, when sunburnt, he was red, not brown; and this became a source of great satisfaction when he learned that Lord Nelson had the same peculiarity. Albert's favorite books were the sea romances of Captain Marryat, whose "Peter Simple" and "Midshipman Easy" he held to be the noblest products of human genius. It was a bitter disappointment to him that his father forbade his going to sea and was educating him to be a "landlubber, " which he had been taught by his boy associates to regard as the most contemptible thing on earth.

Two days before Christmas, Biceps Grimlund was sitting in his room, looking gloomily out of the window. He wished to postpone as long as possible his departure for Aunt Elsbeth's country-place, for he foresaw that both he and she were doomed to a surfeit of each other's company during the coming fortnight. At last he heaved a deep sigh and languidly began to pack his trunk. He had just disposed the dear Marryat books on top of his starched shirts, when he heard rapid footsteps on the stairs, and the next moment the door burst open, and his classmate, Ralph Hoyer, rushed breathlessly into the room.

"Biceps, " he cried, "look at this! Here is a letter from my father, and he tells me to invite one of my classmates to come home with me for the vacation. Will you come? Oh, we shall have grand times, I tell you! No end of fun! "

Albert, instead of answering, jumped up and danced a jig on the floor, upsetting two chairs and breaking the wash-pitcher.

"Hurrah! " he cried, "I'm your man. Shake hands on it, Ralph! You have saved me from two weeks of cats and yarn and moping! Give us your paw! I never was so glad to see anybody in all my life. "

And to prove it, he seized Ralph by the shoulders, gave him a vigorous whirl and forced him to join in the dance.

"Now, stop your nonsense, " Ralph protested, laughing; "if you have so much strength to waste, wait till we are at home in Solheim, and you'll have a chance to use it profitably. "

Albert flung himself down on his old rep-covered sofa. It seemed to have some internal disorder, for its springs rattled and a vague musical twang indicated that something or other had snapped. It had seen much maltreatment, that poor old piece of furniture, and bore visible marks of it. When, after various exhibitions of joy, their boisterous delight had quieted down, both boys began to discuss their plans for the vacation.

"But I fear my groom may freeze, down there in the street, " Ralph ejaculated, cutting short the discussion; "it is bitter cold, and he can't leave the horses. Hurry up, now, old man, and I'll help you pack. "

It did not take them long to complete the packing. Albert sent a telegram to his father, asking permission to accept Ralph's invitation; but, knowing well that the reply would be favorable, did not think it necessary to wait for it. With the assistance of his friend he now wrapped himself in two overcoats, pulled a pair of thick woollen stockings over the outside of his boots and a pair of fur-lined top-boots outside of these, girded himself with three long scarfs, and pulled his brown otter-skin cap down over his ears. He was nearly as broad as he was long, when he had completed these operations, and descended into the street where the big double-sleigh (made in the shape of a huge white swan) was awaiting them. They now called at Ralph's lodgings, whence he presently emerged in a similar Esquimau costume, wearing a wolf-skin coat which left nothing visible except the tip of his nose and the steam of his breath. Then they started off merrily with jingling bells, and waved a farewell toward many a window, wherein were friends and acquaintances. They felt in so jolly a mood, that they could not help shouting their joy in the face of all the world, and crowing over all poor wretches who were left to spend the holidays in the city.

II.

Solheim was about twenty miles from the city, and it was nine o'clock in the evening when the boys arrived there. The moon was shining brightly, and the Milky Way, with its myriad stars, looked like a luminous mist across the vault of the sky. The aurora borealis swept down from the north with white and pink radiations which flushed the dark blue sky for an instant, and vanished. The earth was white, as far as the eye could reach —splendidly, dazzlingly white. And out of the white radiance rose the great dark pile of masonry called Solheim, with its tall chimneys and dormer-windows and old-fashioned gables. Round about stood the tall leafless maples and chestnut-trees, sparkling with frost and stretching their gaunt arms against the heavens. The two horses, when they swung up before the great front-door, were so white with hoar-frost that they looked shaggy like goats, and no one could tell what was their original color. Their breath was blown in two vapory columns from their nostrils and drifted about their heads like steam about a locomotive.

The sleigh-bells had announced the arrival of the guests, and a great shout of welcome was heard from the hall of the house, which seemed alive with grownup people and children. Ralph jumped out of the sleigh, embraced at random half a dozen people, one of whom was his mother, kissed right and left, protesting laughingly against being smothered in affection, and finally managed to introduce his friend, who for the moment was feeling a trifle lonely.

"Here, father, " he cried. "Biceps, this is my father; and, father, this is my Biceps— —"

"What stuff you are talking, boy, " his father exclaimed. "How can this young fellow be your biceps— —"

"Well, how can a man keep his senses in such confusion? " said the son of the house. "This is my friend and classmate, Albert Grimlund, alias Biceps Grimlund, and the strongest man in the whole school. Just feel his biceps, mother, and you'll see. "

"No, I thank you. I'll take your word for it, " replied Mrs. Hoyer. "As I intend to treat him as a friend of my son should be treated, I hope he will not feel inclined to give me any proof of his muscularity. "

When, with the aid of the younger children, the travellers had divested themselves of their various wraps and overcoats, they were ushered into the old-fashioned sitting-room. In one corner roared an enormous, many-storied, iron stove. It had a picture in relief, on one side, of Diana the Huntress, with her nymphs and baying hounds. In the middle of the room stood a big table, and in the middle of the table a big lamp, about which the entire family soon gathered. It was so cosey and homelike that Albert, before he had been half an hour in the room, felt gratefully the atmosphere of mutual affection which pervaded the house. It amused him particularly to watch the little girls, of whom there were six, and to observe their profound admiration for their big brother. Every now and then one of them, sidling up to him while he sat talking, would cautiously touch his ear or a curl of his hair; and if he deigned to take any notice of her, offering her, perhaps, a perfunctory kiss, her pride and pleasure were charming to witness.

Presently the signal was given that supper was ready, and various savory odors, which escaped, whenever a door was opened, served to arouse the anticipations of the boys to the highest pitch. Now, if I did not have so much else to tell you, I should stop here and describe that supper. There were twenty-two people who sat down to it; but that was nothing unusual at Solheim, for it was a hospitable house, where every wayfarer was welcome, either to the table in the servants' hall or to the master's table in the dining-room.

III.

At the stroke of ten all the family arose, and each in turn kissed the father and mother good-night; whereupon Mr. Hoyer took the great lamp from the table and mounted the stairs, followed by his pack of noisy boys and girls. Albert and Ralph found themselves, with four smaller Hoyers, in an enormous low-ceiled room with many windows. In three corners stood huge canopied bedsteads, with flowered-chintz curtains and mountainous eiderdown coverings which swelled up toward the ceiling. In the middle of the wall, opposite the windows, a big iron stove, like the one in the sitting-room (only that it was adorned with a bunch of flowers, peaches, and grapes, and not with Diana and her nymphs), was roaring merrily, and sending a long red sheen from its draught-hole across the floor.

Around the big warm stove the boys gathered (for it was positively Siberian in the region of the windows), and while undressing played various pranks upon each other, which created much merriment. But the most laughter was provoked at the expense of Finn Hoyer, a boy of fourteen, whose bare back his brother insisted upon exhibiting to his guest; for it was decorated with a facsimile of the picture on the stove, showing roses and luscious peaches and grapes in red relief. Three years before, on Christmas Eve, the boys had stood about the red-hot stove, undressing for their bath, and Finn, who was naked, had, in the general scrimmage to get first into the bath-tub, been pushed against the glowing iron, the ornamentation of which had been beautifully burned upon his back. He had to be wrapped in oil and cotton after that adventure, and he recovered in due time, but never quite relished the distinction he had acquired by his pictorial skin.

It was long before Albert fell asleep; for the cold kept up a continual fusillade, as of musketry, during the entire night. The woodwork of the walls snapped and cracked with loud reports; and a little after midnight a servant came in and stuffed the stove full of birch-wood, until it roared like an angry lion. This roar finally lulled Albert to sleep, in spite of the startling noises about him.

The next morning the boys were aroused at seven o'clock by a servant, who brought a tray with the most fragrant coffee and hot rolls. It was in honor of the guest that, in accordance with Norse custom, this early meal was served; and all the boys, carrying pillows and blankets, gathered on Albert's and Ralph's bed and feasted right royally. So it seemed to them, at least; for any break in the ordinary routine, be it ever so slight, is an event to the young. Then they had a pillow-fight, thawed at the stove the water in the pitchers (for it was frozen hard), and arrayed themselves to descend and meet the family at the nine o'clock breakfast. When this repast was at an end, the question arose how they were to entertain their guest, and various plans were proposed. But to all Ralph's propositions his mother interposed the objection that it was too cold.

"Mother is right, " said Mr. Hoyer; "it is so cold that 'the chips jump on the hill-side. ' You'll have to be content with indoor sports to-day."

"But, father, it is not more than twenty degrees below zero, " the boy demurred. "I am sure we can stand that, if we keep in motion. I have been out at thirty without losing either ears or nose. "

He went to the window to observe the thermometer; but the dim daylight scarcely penetrated the fantastic frost-crystals, which, like a splendid exotic flora, covered the panes. Only at the upper corner, where the ice had commenced to thaw, a few timid sunbeams were peeping in, making the lamp upon the table seem pale and sickly. Whenever the door to the hall was opened a white cloud of vapor rolled in; and every one made haste to shut the door, in order to save the precious heat. The boys, being doomed to remain indoors, walked about restlessly, felt each other's muscle, punched each other, and sometimes, for want of better employment, teased the little girls. Mr. Hoyer, seeing how miserable they were, finally took pity on them, and, after having thawed out a window-pane sufficiently to see the thermometer outside, gave his consent to a little expedition on skees[2] down to the river.

[2] Norwegian snow-shoes.

And now, boys, you ought to have seen them! Now there was life in them! You would scarcely have dreamed that they were the same creatures who, a moment ago, looked so listless and miserable. What rollicking laughter and fun, while they bundled one another in scarfs, cardigan-jackets, fur-lined top-boots, and overcoats!

"You had better take your guns along, boys, " said the father, as they stormed out through the front door; "you might strike a couple of ptarmigan, or a mountain-cock, over on the west side. "

"I am going to take your rifle, if you'll let me, " Ralph exclaimed. "I have a fancy we might strike bigger game than mountain-cock. I shouldn't object to a wolf or two. "

"You are welcome to the rifle, " said his father; "but I doubt whether you'll find wolves on the ice so early in the day. "

Mr. Hoyer took the rifle from its case, examined it carefully, and handed it to Ralph. Albert, who was a less experienced hunter than Ralph, preferred a fowling-piece to the rifle; especially as he had no expectation of shooting anything but ptarmigan. Powder-horns, cartridges, and shot were provided; and quite proudly the two friends started off on their skees, gliding over the hard crust of the snow, which, as the sun rose higher, was oversown with thousands of glittering gems. The boys looked like Esquimaux, with their heads bundled up in scarfs, and nothing visible except their eyes and a few hoary locks of hair which the frost had silvered.

IV.

"What was that? " cried Albert, startled by a sharp report which reverberated from the mountains. They had penetrated the forest on the west side, and ranged over the ice for an hour, in a vain search for wolves.

"Hush, " said Ralph, excitedly; and after a moment of intent listening he added, "I'll be drawn and quartered if it isn't poachers! "

"How do you know? "

"These woods belong to father, and no one else has any right to hunt in them. He doesn't mind if a poor man kills a hare or two, or a brace of ptarmigan; but these chaps are after elk; and if the old gentleman gets on the scent of elk-hunters, he has no more mercy than Beelzebub. "

"How can you know that they are after elk? "

"No man is likely to go to the woods for small game on a day like this. They think the cold protects them from pursuit and capture. "

"What are you going to do about it? "

"I am going to play a trick on them. You know that the sheriff, whose duty it is to be on the lookout for elk-poachers, would scarcely send out a posse when the cold is so intense. Elk, you know, are becoming very scarce, and the law protects them. No man is allowed to shoot more than one elf a year, and that one on his own property. Now, you and I will play deputy-sheriffs, and have those poachers securely in the lock-up before night. "

"But suppose they fight? "

"Then we'll fight back. "

Ralph was so aglow with joyous excitement at the thought of this adventure, that Albert had not the heart to throw cold water on his enthusiasm. Moreover, he was afraid of being thought cowardly by his friend if he offered objections. The recollection of Midshipman Easy and his daring pranks flashed through his brain, and he felt an instant desire to rival the exploits of his favorite hero. If only the enterprise had been on the sea he would have been twice as happy, for the land always seemed to him a prosy and inconvenient place for the exhibition of heroism.

"But, Ralph, " he exclaimed, now more than ready to bear his part in the expedition, "I have only shot in my gun. You can't shoot men with bird-shot. "

"Shoot men! Are you crazy? Why, I don't intend to shoot anybody.

I only wish to capture them. My rifle is a breech-loader and has six cartridges. Besides, it has twice the range of theirs (for there isn't another such rifle in all Odalen), and by firing one shot over their heads I can bring them to terms, don't you see? "

Albert, to be frank, did not see it exactly; but he thought it best to suppress his doubts. He scented danger in the air, and his blood bounded through his veins.

"How do you expect to track them? " he asked, breathlessly.

"Skee-tracks in the snow can be seen by a bat, born blind, " answered Ralph, recklessly.

They were now climbing up the wooded slope on the western side of the river. The crust of the frozen snow was strong enough to bear them; and as it was not glazed, but covered with an inch of hoar-frost, it retained the imprint of their feet with distinctness. They were obliged to carry their skees, on account both of the steepness of the slope and the density of the underbrush. Roads and paths were invisible under the white pall of the snow, and only the facility with which they could retrace their steps saved them from the fear of going astray. Through the vast forest a deathlike silence reigned; and this silence was not made up of an infinity of tiny sounds, like the silence of a summer day when the crickets whirr in the treetops and the bees drone in the clover-blossoms. No; this silence was dead, chilling, terrible. The huge pine-trees now and then dropped a load of snow on the heads of the bold intruders, and it fell with a thud, followed by a noiseless, glittering drizzle. As far as their eyes could reach, the monotonous colonnade of brown tree-trunks, rising out of the white waste, extended in all directions. It reminded them of the enchanted forest in "Undine, " through which a man might ride forever without finding the end. It was a great relief when, from time to time, they met a squirrel out foraging for pine-cones or picking up a scanty living among the husks of last year's hazel-nuts. He was lively in spite of the weather, and the faint noises of his small activities fell gratefully upon ears already ap-palled by the awful silence. Occasionally they scared up a brace of grouse that seemed half benumbed, and hopped about in a melancholy manner under the pines, or a magpie, drawing in its head and ruffling up its feathers against the cold, until it looked frowsy and disreputable.

"Biceps, " whispered Ralph, who had suddenly discovered something interesting in the snow, "do you see that? "

"Je-rusalem! " ejaculated Albert, with thoughtless delight, "it is a hoof-track! "

"Hold your tongue, you blockhead, " warned his friend, too excited to be polite, "or you'll spoil the whole business! "

"But you asked me, " protested Albert, in a huff.

"But I didn't shout, did I? "

Again the report of a shot tore a great rent in the wintry stillness and rang out with sharp reverberations.

"We've got them, " said Ralph, examining the lock of his rifle. "That shot settles them. "

"If we don't look out, they may get us instead, " grumbled Albert, who was still offended.

Ralph stood peering into the underbrush, his eyes as wild as those of an Indian, his nostrils dilated, and all his senses intensely awake. His companion, who was wholly unskilled in woodcraft, could see no cause for his agitation, and feared that he was yet angry. He did not detect the evidences of large game in the immediate neighborhood. He did not see, by the bend of the broken twigs and the small tufts of hair on the briar-bush, that an elk had pushed through that very copse within a few minutes; nor did he sniff the gamy odor with which the large beast had charged the air. In obedience to his friend's gesture, he flung himself down on hands and knees and cautiously crept after him through the thicket. He now saw without difficulty a place where the elk had broken through the snow crust, and he could also detect a certain aimless bewilderment in the tracks, owing, no doubt, to the shot and the animal's perception of danger on two sides. Scarcely had he crawled twenty feet when he was startled by a noise of breaking branches, and before he had time to cock his gun, he saw an enormous bull-elk tearing through the underbrush, blowing two columns of steam from his nostrils, and steering straight toward them. At the same instant Ralph's rifle blazed away, and the splendid beast, rearing on its hind legs, gave a wild snort, plunged forward and rolled on its side in the snow. Quick as a flash the young hunter had drawn his knife, and, in accordance with the laws of the chase, had driven it into the breast of the animal. But the glance from the dying eyes—that glance, of which every elk-hunter can tell a moving tale—pierced the boy to the very heart! It was such a touching, appealing, imploring glance, so soft and gentle and unresentful.

"Why did you harm me, " it seemed to say, "who never harmed any living thing—who claimed only the right to live my frugal life in the forest, digging up the frozen mosses under the snow, which no mortal creature except myself can eat? "

The sanguinary instinct—the fever for killing, which every boy inherits from savage ancestors—had left Ralph, before he had pulled the knife from the bleeding wound. A miserable feeling of guilt stole over him. He never had shot an elk before; and his father, who was anxious to preserve the noble beasts from destruction, had not availed himself of his right to kill one for many years. Ralph had, indeed, many a time hunted rabbits, hares, mountain-cock, and capercaillie. But they had never destroyed his pleasure by arousing pity for their deaths; and he had always regarded himself as being proof against sentimental emotions.

"Look here, Biceps, " he said, flinging the knife into the snow, "I wish I hadn't killed that bull. "

"I thought we were hunting for poachers, " answered Albert, dubiously; "and now we have been poaching ourselves. "

"By Jiminy! So we have; and I never once thought of it, " cried the valiant hunter. "I am afraid we are off my father's preserves too. It is well the deputy sheriffs are not abroad, or we might find ourselves decorated with iron bracelets before night. "

"But what did you do it for? "

"Well, I can't tell. It's in the blood, I fancy. The moment I saw the track and caught the wild smell, I forgot all about the poachers, and started on the scent like a hound. "

The two boys stood for some minutes looking at the dead animal, not with savage exultation, but with a dim regret. The blood which was gushing from the wound in the breast froze in a solid lump the very moment it touched the snow, although the cold had greatly moderated since the morning.

"I suppose we'll have to skin the fellow, " remarked Ralph, lugubriously; "it won't do to leave that fine carcass for the wolves to celebrate Christmas with. "

"All right, " Albert answered, "I am not much of a hand at skinning, but I'll do the best I can. "

They fell to work rather reluctantly at the unwonted task, but had not proceeded far when they perceived that they had a full day's job before them.

"I've no talent for the butcher's trade, " Ralph exclaimed in disgust, dropping his knife into the snow. "There's no help for it, Biceps, we'll have to bury the carcass, pile some logs on the top of it, and send a horse to drag it home to-morrow. If it were not Christmas Eve to-night we might take a couple of men along and shoot a dozen wolves or more. For there is sure to be pandemonium here before long, and a concert in G-flat that'll curdle the marrow of your bones with horror. "

"Thanks, " replied the admirer of Midshipman Easy, striking a reckless naval attitude. "The marrow of my bones is not so easily curdled. I've been on a whaling voyage, which is more than you have. "

Ralph was about to vindicate his dignity by referring to his own valiant exploits, when suddenly his keen eyes detected a slight motion in the underbrush on the slope below.

"Biceps, " he said, with forced composure, "those poachers are tracking us. "

"What do you mean? " asked Albert, in vague alarm.

"Do you see the top of that young birch waving? "

"Well, what of that! "

"Wait and see. It's no good trying to escape. They can easily overtake us. The snow is the worst tell-tale under the sun. "

"But why should we wish to escape? I thought we were going to catch them. "

"So we were; but that was before we turned poachers ourselves. Now those fellows will turn the tables on us—take us to the sheriff and collect half the fine, which is fifty dollars, as informers. "

"Je-rusalem! " cried Biceps, "isn't it a beautiful scrape we've gotten into? "

"Rather, " responded his friend, coolly.

"But why meekly allow ourselves to be captured? Why not defend ourselves? "

"My dear Biceps, you don't know what you are talking about. Those fellows don't mind putting a bullet into you, if you run. Now, I'd rather pay fifty dollars any day, than shoot a man even in self-defence. "

"But they have killed elk too. We heard them shoot twice. Suppose we play the same game on them that they intend to play on us. We can play informers too, then we'll at least be quits. "

"Biceps, you are a brick! That's a capital idea! Then let us start for the sheriff's; and if we get there first, we'll inform both on ourselves and on them. That'll cancel the fine. Quick, now! "

No persuasions were needed to make Albert bestir himself. He leaped toward his skees, and following his friend, who was a few rods ahead of him, started down the slope in a zigzag line, cautiously steering his way among the tree trunks. The boys had taken their departure none too soon; for they were scarcely five hundred yards down the declivity, when they heard behind them loud exclamations and oaths. Evidently the poachers had stopped to roll some logs (which were lying close by) over the carcass, probably meaning to appropriate it; and this gave the boys an advantage, of which they were in great need. After a few moments they espied an open clearing which sloped steeply down toward the river. Toward this Ralph had been directing his course; for although it was a venturesome undertaking to slide down so steep and rugged a hill, he was determined rather to break his neck than lower his pride, and become the laughing-stock of the parish.

One more tack through alder copse and juniper jungle—hard indeed, and terribly vexatious—and he saw with delight the great open slope, covered with an unbroken surface of glittering snow. The sun (which at midwinter is but a few hours above the horizon) had set; and the stars were flashing forth with dazzling brilliancy. Ralph stopped, as he reached the clearing, to give Biceps an opportunity to overtake him; for Biceps, like all marine animals, moved with less dexterity on the dry land.

"Ralph, " he whispered breathlessly, as he pushed himself up to his companion with a vigorous thrust of his skee-staff, "there are two awful chaps close behind us. I distinctly heard them speak. "

"Fiddlesticks, " said Ralph; "now let us see what you are made of!

Don't take my track, or you may impale me like a roast pig on a spit. Now, ready! —one, two, three! "

"Hold on there, or I shoot, " yelled a hoarse voice from out of the underbrush; but it was too late; for at the same instant the two boys slid out over the steep slope, and, wrapped in a whirl of loose snow, were scudding at a dizzying speed down the precipitous hill-side. Thump, thump, thump, they went, where hidden wood-piles or fences obstructed their path, and out they shot into space, but each time came down firmly on their feet, and dashed ahead with undiminished ardor. Their calves ached, the cold air whistled in their ears, and their eyelids became stiff and their sight half obscured with the hoar-frost that fringed their lashes. But onward they sped, keeping their balance with wonderful skill, until they reached the gentler slope which formed the banks of the great river. Then for the first time Ralph had an opportunity to look behind him, and he saw two moving whirls of snow darting downward, not far from his own track. His heart beat in his throat; for those fellows had both endurance and skill, and he feared that he was no match for them. But suddenly—he could have yelled with delight—the foremost figure leaped into the air, turned a tremendous somersault, and, coming down on his head, broke through the crust of the snow and vanished, while his skees started on an independent journey down the hill-side. He had struck an exposed fence-rail, which, abruptly checking his speed, had sent him flying like a rocket.

The other poacher had barely time to change his course, so as to avoid the snag; but he was unable to stop and render assistance to his fallen comrade. The boys, just as they were shooting out upon the ice, saw by his motions that he was hesitating whether or not he should give up the chase. He used his staff as a brake for a few moments, so as to retard his speed; but discovering, perhaps, by the brightening starlight, that his adversaries were not full-grown men, he took courage, started forward again, and tried to make up for the time he had lost. If he could but reach the sheriff's house before the boys did, he could have them arrested and collect the informer's fee, instead of being himself arrested and fined as a poacher. It was a prize worth racing for! And, moreover, there were two elks, worth twenty-five dollars apiece, buried in the snow under logs. These also would belong to the victor! The poacher dashed ahead, straining every nerve, and reached safely the foot of the steep declivity. The boys were now but a few hundred yards ahead of him.

"Hold on there, " he yelled again, "or I shoot! "

He was not within range, but he thought he could frighten the youngsters into abandoning the race. The sheriff's house was but a short distance up the river. Its tall, black chimneys could he seen looming up against the starlit sky. There was no slope now to accelerate their speed. They had to peg away for dear life, pushing themselves forward with their skee-staves, laboring like plough-horses, panting, snorting, perspiring. Ralph turned his head once more. The poacher was gaining upon them; there could be no doubt of it. He was within the range of Ralph's rifle; and a sturdy fellow he was, who seemed good for a couple of miles yet. Should Ralph send a bullet over his head to frighten him? No; that might give the poacher an excuse for sending back a bullet with a less innocent purpose. Poor Biceps, he was panting and puffing in his heavy wraps like a steamboat! He did not once open his mouth to speak; but, exerting his vaunted muscle to the utmost, kept abreast of his friend, and sometimes pushed a pace or two ahead of him. But it cost him a mighty effort! And yet the poacher was gaining upon him! They could see the long broadside of windows in the sheriff's mansion, ablaze with Christmas candles. They came nearer and nearer! The church-bells up on the bend were ringing in the festival. Five minutes more and they would be at their goal. Five minutes more! Surely they had strength enough left for that small space of time. So had the poacher, probably! The question was, which had the most. Then, with a short, sharp resonance, followed by a long reverberation, a shot rang out and a bullet whizzed past Ralph's ear. It was the poacher who had broken the peace. Ralph, his blood boiling with wrath, came to a sudden stop, flung his rifle to his cheek and cried, "Drop that gun! "

The poacher, bearing down with all his might on the skee-staff, checked his speed. In the meanwhile Albert hurried on, seeing that the issue of the race depended upon him.

"Don't force me to hurt ye! " shouted the poacher, threateningly, to Ralph, taking aim once more.

"You can't, " Ralph shouted back. "You haven't another shot. "

At that instant sounds of sleigh-bells and voices were heard, and half a dozen people, startled by the shot, were seen rushing out from the sheriff's mansion. Among them was Mr. Bjornerud himself, with one of his deputies.

"In the name of the law, I command you to cease, " he cried, when he saw down the two figures in menacing attitudes. But before he could say another word, some one fell prostrate in the road before him, gasping:

"We have shot an elk; so has that man down on the ice. We give ourselves up. "

Mr. Bjornerud, making no answer, leaped over the prostrate figure, and, followed by the deputy, dashed down upon the ice.

"In the name of the law! " he shouted again, and both rifles were reluctantly lowered.

"I have shot an elk, " cried Ralph, eagerly, "and this man is a poacher, we heard him shoot. "

"I have killed an elk, " screamed the poacher, in the same moment, "and so has this fellow. "

The sheriff was too astonished to speak. Never before, in his experience, had poachers raced for dear life to give themselves into custody. He feared that they were making sport of him; in that case, however, he resolved to make them suffer for their audacity.

"You are my prisoners, " he said, after a moment's hesitation. "Take them to the lock-up, Olsen, and handcuff them securely, " he added, turning to his deputy.

There were now a dozen men — most of them guests and attendants of the sheriff's household — standing in a ring about Ralph and the poacher. Albert, too, had scrambled to his feet and had joined his comrade.

"Will you permit me, Mr. Sheriff, " said Ralph, making the officer his politest bow, "to send a message to my father, who is probably anxious about us? "

"And who is your father, young man? " asked the sheriff, not unkindly; "I should think you were doing him an ill-turn in taking to poaching at your early age. "

"My father is Mr. Hoyer, of Solheim, " said the boy, not without some pride in the announcement.

"What—you rascal, you! Are you trying to, play pranks on an old man? " cried the officer of the law, grasping Ralph cordially by the hand. "You've grown to be quite a man, since I saw you last. Pardon me for not recognizing the son of an old neighbor. "

"Allow me to introduce to you my friend, Mr. Biceps—I mean, Mr. Albert Grimlund. "

"Happy to make your acquaintance, Mr. Biceps Albert; and now you must both come and eat the Christmas porridge with us. I'll send a messenger to Mr. Hoyer without delay. "

The sheriff, in a jolly mood, and happy to have added to the number of his Christmas guests, took each of the two young men by the arm, as if he were going to arrest them, and conducted them through the spacious front hall into a large cosey room, where, having divested themselves of their wraps, they told the story of their adventure.

"But, my dear sir, " Mr. Bjornerud exclaimed, "I don't see how you managed to go beyond your father's preserves. You know he bought of me the whole forest tract, adjoining his own on the south, about three months ago. So you were perfectly within your rights; for your father hasn't killed an elk on his land for three years. "

"If that is the case, Mr. Sheriff, " said Ralph, "I must beg of you to release the poor fellow who chased us. I don't wish any informer's fee, nor have I any desire to get him into trouble. "

"I am sorry to say I can't accommodate you, " Bjornerud replied. "This man is a notorious poacher and trespasser, whom my deputies have long been tracking in vain. Now that I have him I shall keep him. There's no elk safe in Odalen so long as that rascal is at large. "

"That may be; but I shall then turn my informer's fee over to him, which will reduce his fine from fifty dollars to twenty-five dollars. "

"To encourage him to continue poaching? "

"Well, I confess I have a little more sympathy with poachers, since we came so near being poachers ourselves. It was only an accident that saved us! "

THE NIXY'S STRAIN

Little Nils had an idea that he wanted to be something great in the world, but he did not quite know how to set about it. He had always been told that, having been born on a Sunday, he was a luck-child, and that good fortune would attend him on that account in whatever he undertook.

He had never, so far, noticed anything peculiar about himself, though, to be sure, his small enterprises did not usually come to grief, his snares were seldom empty, and his tiny stamping-mill, which he and his friend Thorstein had worked at so faithfully, was now making a merry noise over in the brook in the Westmo Glen, so that you could hear it a hundred yards away.

The reason of this, his mother told him, according to the superstition of her people, was that the Nixy and the Hulder[3] and the gnomes favored him because he was a Sunday child. What was more, she assured him, that he would see them some day, and then, if he conducted himself cleverly, so as to win their favor, he would, by their aid, rise high in the world, and make his fortune.

[3] The genius of cattle, represented as a beautiful maiden disfigured by a heifer's tail, which she is always trying to hide, though often unsuccessfully.

Now this was exactly what Nils wanted, and therefore he was not a little anxious to catch a glimpse of the mysterious creatures who had so whimsical a reason for taking an interest in him. Many and many a time he sat at the waterfall where the Nixy was said to play the harp every midsummer night, but although he sometimes imagined that he heard a vague melody trembling through the rush and roar of the water, and saw glimpses of white limbs flashing through the current, yet never did he get a good look at the Nixy.

Though he roamed through the woods early and late, setting snares for birds and rabbits, and was ever on the alert for a sight of the Hulder's golden hair and scarlet bodice, the tricksy sprite persisted in eluding him.

He thought sometimes that he heard a faint, girlish giggle, full of teasing provocation and suppressed glee, among the underbrush, and once he imagined that he saw a gleam of scarlet and gold vanish in a dense alder copse.

But very little good did that do him, when he could not fix the vision, talk with it face to face, and extort the fulfilment of the three regulation wishes.

"I am probably not good enough, " thought Nils. "I know I am a selfish fellow, and cruel, too, some-times, to birds and beasts. I suppose she won't have anything to do with me, as long as she isn't satisfied with my behavior. "

Then he tried hard to be kind and considerate; smiled at his little sister when she pulled his hair, patted Sultan, the dog, instead of kicking him, when he was in his way, and never complained or sulked when he was sent on errands late at night or in bad weather.

But, strange to say, though the Nixy's mysterious melody still sounded vaguely through the water's roar, and the Hulder seemed to titter behind the tree-trunks and vanish in the underbrush, a real, unmistakable view was never vouchsafed to Nils, and the three wishes which were to make his fortune he had no chance of propounding.

He had fully made up his mind what his wishes were to be, for he was determined not to be taken by surprise. He knew well the fate of those foolish persons in the fairy tales who offend their benevolent protectors by bouncing against them head foremost, as it were, with a greedy cry for wealth.

Nils was not going to be caught that way. He would ask first for wisdom—that was what all right-minded heroes did—then for good repute among men, and lastly—and here was the rub—lastly he was inclined to ask for a five-bladed knife, like the one the parson's Thorwald had got for a Christmas present.

But he had considerable misgiving about the expediency of this last wish. If he had a fair renown and wisdom, might he not be able to get along without a five-bladed pocket-knife? But no; there was no help for it. Without that five-bladed pocket-knife neither wisdom nor fame would satisfy him. It would be the drop of gall in his cup of joy.

After many days' pondering, it occurred to him, as a way out of the difficulty, that it would, perhaps, not offend the Hulder if he asked, not for wealth, but for a moderate prosperity. If he were blessed with a moderate prosperity, he could, of course, buy a five-bladed pocket-knife with corkscrew and all other appurtenances, and still have something left over.

He had a dreadful struggle with this question, for he was well aware that the proper things to wish were long life and happiness for his father and mother, or something in that line. But, though he wished his father and mother well, he could not make up his mind to forego his own precious chances on their account. Moreover, he consoled himself with the reflection that if he attained the goal of his own desires he could easily bestow upon them, of his bounty, a reasonable prospect of long life and happiness.

You see Nils was by no means so good yet as he ought to be. He was clever enough to perceive that he had small chance of seeing the Hulder, as long as his heart was full of selfishness and envy and greed.

For, strive as he might, he could not help feeling envious of the parson's Thorwald, with his elaborate combination pocket-knife and his silver watch-chain, which he unfeelingly flaunted in the face of an admiring community. It was small consolation for Nils to know that there was no watch but only a key attached to it; for a silver watch-chain, even without a watch, was a sufficiently splendid possession to justify a boy in fording it over his less fortunate comrades.

Nils's father, who was a poor charcoal-burner, could never afford to make his son such a present, even if he worked until he was as black as a chimney-sweep. For what little money he earned was needed at once for food and clothes for the family; and there were times when they were obliged to mix ground birch-bark with their flour in order to make it last longer.

It was easy enough for a rich man's son to be good, Nils thought.

It was small credit to him if he was not envious, having never known want and never gone to bed on birch-bark porridge. But for a poor boy not to covet all the nice things which would make life so pleasant, if he had them, seemed next to impossible.

Still Nils kept on making good resolutions and breaking them, and then piecing them together again and breaking them anew.

If it had not been for his desire to see the Hulder and the Nixy, and making them promise the fulfilment of the three wishes, he would have given up the struggle, and resigned himself to being a bad boy because he was born so. But those teasing glimpses of the Hulder's scarlet bodice and golden hair, and the vague snatches of wondrous melody that rose from the cataract in the silent summer nights, filled his soul with an intense desire to see the whole Hulder, with her radiant smile and melancholy eyes, and to hear the whole melody plainly enough to be written down on paper and learned by heart.

It was with this longing to repeat the few haunting notes that hummed in his brain that Nils went to the schoolmaster one day and asked him for the loan of his fiddle. But the schoolmaster, hearing that Nils could not play, thought his request a foolish one and refused.

Nevertheless, that visit became an important event, and a turning-point in the boy's life. For he was moved to confide in the schoolmaster, who was a kindly old man, and fond of clever boys; and he became interested in Nils. Though he regarded Nils's desire to record the Nixy's strains as absurd, he offered to teach him to play. There was good stuff in the lad, he thought, and when he had out-grown his fantastic nonsense, he might, very likely, make a good fiddler.

Thus it came to pass that the charcoal-burner's son learned to play the violin. He had not had half a dozen lessons before he set about imitating the Nixy's notes which he had heard in the waterfall.

"It was this way, " he said to the schoolmaster, pressing his ear against the violin, while he ran the bow lightly over the strings; "or rather it was this way, " making another ineffectual effort. "No, no, that wasn't it, either. It's no use, schoolmaster: I shall never be able to do it! " he cried, flinging the violin on the table and rushing out of the door.

When he returned the next day he was heartily ashamed of his impatience. To try to catch the Nixy's notes after half a dozen lessons was, of course, an absurdity.

The master told him simply to banish such folly from his brain, to apply himself diligently to his scales, and not to bother himself about the Nixy.

That seemed to be sound advice and Nils accepted it with contrition. He determined never to repeat his silly experiment. But when the next midsummer night came, a wild yearning possessed him, and he stole out noiselessly into the forest, and sat down on a stone by the river, listening intently.

For a long while he heard nothing but the monotonous boom of the water plunging into the deep. But, strangely enough, there was a vague, hushed rhythm in this thundering roar; and after a while he seemed to hear a faint strain, ravishingly sweet, which vibrated on the air for an instant and vanished.

It seemed to steal upon his ear unawares, and the moment he listened, with a determination to catch it, it was gone. But sweet it was—inexpressibly sweet.

Let the master talk as much as he liked, catch it he would and catch it he must. But he must acquire greater skill before he would be able to render something so delicate and elusive.

Accordingly Nils applied himself with all his might and main to his music, in the intervals between his work.

He was big enough now to accompany his father to the woods, and help him pile turf and earth on the heap of logs that were to be burned to charcoal. He did not see the Hulder face to face, though he was constantly on the watch for her; but once or twice he thought he saw a swift flash of scarlet and gold in the underbrush, and again and again he thought he heard her soft, teasing laughter in the alder copses. That, too, he imagined he might express in music; and the next time he got hold of the schoolmaster's fiddle he quavered away on the fourth string, but produced nothing that had the remotest resemblance to melody, much less to that sweet laughter.

He grew so discouraged that he could have wept. He had a wild impulse to break the fiddle, and never touch another as long as he lived. But he knew he could not live up to any such resolution. The fiddle was already too dear to him to be renounced for a momentary whim. But it was like an unrequited affection, which brought as much sorrow as joy.

There was so much that Nils burned to express; but the fiddle refused to obey him, and screeched something utterly discordant, as it seemed, from sheer perversity.

It occurred to Nils again, that unless the Nixy took pity on him and taught him that marvellous, airy strain he would never catch it. Would he then ever be good enough to win the favor of the Nixy?

For in the fairy tales it is always the bad people who come to grief, while the good and merciful ones are somehow rewarded.

It was evidently because he was yet far from being good enough that both Hulder and Nixy eluded him. Sunday child though he was, there seemed to be small chance that he would ever be able to propound his three wishes.

Only now, the third wish was no longer a five-bladed pocket-knife, but a violin of so fine a ring and delicate modulation that it might render the Nixy's strain.

While these desires and fancies fought in his heart, Nils grew to be a young man; and he still was, what he had always been—a charcoal-burner. He went to the parson for half a year to prepare for confirmation; and by his gentleness and sweetness of disposition attracted not only the good man himself, but all with whom he came in contact. His answers were always thoughtful, and betrayed a good mind.

He was not a prig, by any means, who held aloof from sport and play; he could laugh with the merriest, run a race with the swiftest, and try a wrestling match with the strongest.

There was no one among the candidates for confirmation, that year, who was so well liked as Nils. Gentle as he was and soft-spoken, there was a manly spirit in him, and that always commands respect among boys.

He received much praise from the pastor, and no one envied him the kind words that were addressed to him; for every one felt that they were deserved. But the thought in Nils's mind during all the ceremony in the church and in the parsonage was this:

"Now, perhaps, I shall be good enough to win the Nixy's favor. Now I shall catch the wondrous strain. "

It did not occur to him, in his eagerness, that such a reflection was out of place in church; nor was it, perhaps, for the Nixy's strain was constantly associated in his mind with all that was best in him; with his highest aspirations, and his constant strivings for goodness and nobleness in thought and deed.

It happened about this time that the old schoolmaster died, and in his will it was found that he had bequeathed his fiddle to Nils. He had very little else to leave, poor fellow; but if he had been a Croesus he could not have given his favorite pupil anything that would have delighted him more.

Nils played now early and late, except when he was in the woods with his father. His fame went abroad through all the valley as the best fiddler in seven parishes round, and people often came from afar to hear him. There was a peculiar quality in his playing—something strangely appealing, that brought the tears to one's eyes—yet so elusive that it was impossible to repeat or describe it.

It was rumored among the villagers that he had caught the Nixy's strain, and that it was that which touched the heart so deeply in his improvisations. But Nils knew well that he had not caught the Nixy's strain; though a faint echo—a haunting undertone—of that vaguely remembered snatch of melody, heard now and then in the water's roar, would steal at times into his music, when he was, perhaps, himself least aware of it.

Invitations now came to him from far and wide to play at wedding and dancing parties and funerals. There was no feast complete without Nils; and soon this strange thing was noticed, that quarrels and brawls, which in those days were common enough in Norway, were rare wherever Nils played.

It seemed as if his calm and gentle presence called forth all that was good in the feasters and banished whatever was evil. Such was his popularity that he earned more money by his fiddling in a week than his father had ever done by charcoal-burning in a month.

A half-superstitious regard for him became general among the people; first, because it seemed impossible that any man could play as he did without the aid of some supernatural power; and secondly, because his gentle demeanor and quaint, terse sayings inspired them with admiration. It was difficult to tell by whom the name, Wise Nils, was first started, but it was felt by all to be appropriate, and it therefore clung to the modest fiddler, in spite of all his protests.

Before he was twenty-five years old it became the fashion to go to him and consult him in difficult situations; and though he long shrank from giving advice, his reluctance wore away, when it became evident to him that he could actually benefit the people.

There was nothing mysterious in his counsel. All he said was as clear and rational as the day-light. But the good folk were nevertheless inclined to attribute a higher authority to him; and would desist from vice or folly for his sake, when they would not for their own sake. It was odd, indeed: this Wise Nils, the fiddler, became a great man in the valley, and his renown went abroad and brought him visitors, seeking his counsel, from distant parishes. Rarely did anyone leave him disappointed, or at least without being benefited by his sympathetic advice.

One summer, during the tourist season, a famous foreign musician came to Norway, accompanied by a rich American gentleman. While in his neighborhood, they heard the story of the rustic fiddler, and became naturally curious to see him.

They accordingly went to his cottage, in order to have some sport with him, for they expected to find a vain and ignorant charlatan, inflated by the flattery of his more ignorant neighbors. But Nils received them with a simple dignity which quite disarmed them. They had come to mock; they stayed to admire. This peasant's artless speech, made up of ancient proverbs and shrewd common-sense, and instinct with a certain sunny beneficence, impressed them wonderfully.

And when, at their request, he played some of his improvisations, the renowned musician exclaimed that here was, indeed, a great artist lost to the world. In spite of the poor violin, there was a marvellously touching quality in the music; something new and alluring which had never been heard before.

But Nils himself was not aware of it. Occasionally, while he played, the Nixy's haunting strain would flit through his brain, or hover about it, where he could feel it, as it were, but yet be unable to catch it. This was his regret—his constant chase for those elusive notes that refused to be captured.

But he consoled himself many a time with the reflection that it was the fiddle's fault, not his own. With a finer instrument, capable of rendering more delicate shades of sound, he might yet surprise the Nixy's strain, and record it unmistakably in black and white.

The foreign musician and his American friend departed, but returned at the end of two weeks. They then offered to accompany Nils on a concert tour through all the capitals of Europe and the large cities of America, and to insure him a sum of money which fairly made him dizzy.

Nils begged for time to consider, and the next day surprised them by declining the startling offer.

He was a peasant, he said, and must remain a peasant. He belonged here in his native valley, where he could do good, and was happy in the belief that he was useful.

Out in the great world, of which he knew nothing, he might indeed gather wealth, but he might lose his peace of mind, which was more precious than wealth. He was content with a moderate prosperity, and that he had already attained. He had enough, and more than enough, to satisfy his modest wants, and to provide those who were dear to him with reasonable comfort in their present condition of life.

The strangers were amazed at a man's thus calmly refusing a fortune that was within his easy grasp, for they did not doubt that Nils, with his entirely unconventional manner of playing, and yet with that extraordinary moving quality in his play, would become the rage both in Europe and America, as a kind of heaven-born, untutored genius, and fill both his own pockets and theirs with shekels.

They made repeated efforts to persuade him, but it was all in vain. With smiling serenity, he told them that he had uttered his final decision. They then took leave of him, and a month after their departure there arrived from Germany a box addressed to Nils. He opened it with some trepidation, and it was found to contain a Cremona violin —a genuine Stradivarius.

The moment Nils touched the strings with the bow, a thrill of rapture went through him, the like of which he had never experienced. The divine sweetness and purity of the tone that vibrated through those magic chambers resounded through all his being, and made him feel happy and exalted.

It occurred to him, while he was coaxing the intoxicating music from his instrument, that tonight would be midsummer night. Now was his chance to catch the Nixy's strain, for this exquisite violin would be capable of rendering the very chant of the archangels in the morning of time.

To-night he would surprise the Nixy, and the divine strain should no more drift like a melodious mist through his brain; for at midsummer night the Nixy always plays the loudest, and then, if ever, is the time to learn what he felt must be the highest secret of the musical art.

Hugging his Stradivarius close to his breast, to protect it from the damp night-air, Nils hurried through the birch woods down to the river. The moon was sailing calmly through a fleecy film of cloud, and a light mist hovered over the tops of the forest.

The fiery afterglow of the sunset still lingered in the air, though the sun had long been hidden, but the shadows of the trees were gaunt and dark, as in the light of the moon.

The sound of the cataract stole with a whispering rush through the underbrush, for the water was low at midsummer, and a good deal of it was diverted to the mill, which was working busily away, with its big water-wheel going round and round.

Nils paused close to the mill, and peered intently into the rushing current; but nothing appeared. Then he stole down to the river-bank, where he seated himself on a big stone, barely out of reach of the spray, which blew in gusts from the cataract. He sat for a long while motionless, gazing with rapt intentness at the struggling, foaming rapids, but he saw or heard nothing.

Then all of a sudden it seemed to him that the air began to vibrate faintly with a vague, captivating rhythm. Nils could hear his heart beat in his throat. With trembling eagerness he unwrapped the violin and raised it to his chin.

Now, surely, there was a note. It belonged on the A string. No, not there. On the E string, perhaps. But no, not there, either.

Look! What is that?

A flash, surely, through the water of a beautiful naked arm.

And there—no, not there—but somewhere from out of the gentle rush of the middle current there seemed to come to him a marvellous mist of drifting sound—ineffably, rapturously sweet!

With a light movement Nils runs his bow over the strings, but not a ghost, not a semblance, can he reproduce of the swift, scurrying flight of that wondrous melody. Again and again he listens breathlessly, and again and again despair overwhelms him.

Should he, then, never see the Nixy, and ask the fulfilment of his three wishes?

Curiously enough, those three wishes which once were so great a part of his life had now almost escaped him. It was the Nixy's strain he had been intent upon, and the wishes had lapsed into oblivion.

And what were they, really, those three wishes, for the sake of which he desired to confront the Nixy?

Well, the first—the first was—what was it, now? Yes, now at length he remembered. The first was wisdom.

Well, the people called him Wise Nils now, so, perhaps, that wish was superfluous. Very likely he had as much wisdom as was good for him. At all events, he had refused to acquire more by going abroad to acquaint himself with the affairs of the great world.

Then the second wish; yes, he could recall that. It was fame. It was odd indeed; that, too, he had refused, and what he possessed of it was as much, or even far more, than he desired. But when he called to mind the third and last of his boyish wishes, a moderate prosperity or a good violin—for that was the alternative—he had to laugh outright, for both the violin and the prosperity were already his.

Nils lapsed into deep thought, as he sat there in the summer night, with the crowns of the trees above him and the brawling rapids swirling about him.

Had not the Nixy bestowed upon him her best gift already in permitting him to hear that exquisite ghost of a melody, that shadowy, impalpable strain, which had haunted him these many years? In pursuing that he had gained the goal of his desires, till other things he had wished for had come to him unawares, as it were, and almost without his knowing it. And now what had he to ask of the Nixy, who had blessed him so abundantly?

The last secret, the wondrous strain, forsooth, that he might imprison it in notes, and din it in the ears of an unappreciative multitude! Perhaps it were better, after all, to persevere forever in the quest, for what would life have left to offer him if the Nixy's strain was finally caught, when all were finally attained, and no divine melody haunted the brain, beyond the powers even of a Stradivarius to lure from its shadowy realm?

Nils walked home that night plunged in deep meditation. He vowed to himself that he would never more try to catch the Nixy's strain. But the next day, when he seized the violin, there it was again, and, strive as he might, he could not forbear trying to catch it.

Wise Nils is many years older now; has a good wife and several children, and is a happy man; but to this day, resolve as he will, he has never been able to abandon the effort to catch the Nixy's strain. Sometimes he thinks he has half caught it, but when he tries to play it, it is always gone.

THE WONDER CHILD

I.

A very common belief in Norway, as in many other lands, is that the seventh child of the seventh child can heal the sick by the laying on of hands. Such a child is therefore called a wonder child. Little Carina Holt was the seventh in a family of eight brothers and sisters, but she grew to be six years old before it became generally known that she was a wonder child. Then people came from afar to see her, bringing their sick with them; and morning after morning, as Mrs. Holt rolled up the shades, she found invalids, seated or standing in the snow, gazing with devout faith and anxious longing toward Carina's window.

It seemed a pity to send them away uncomforted, when the look and the touch cost Carina so little. But there was another fear that arose in the mother's breast, and that was lest her child should be harmed by the veneration with which she was regarded, and perhaps come to believe that she was something more than a common mortal. What was more natural than that a child who was told by grown-up people that there was healing in her touch, should at last come to believe that she was something apart and extraordinary?

It would have been a marvel, indeed, if the constant attention she attracted, and the pilgrimages that were made to her, had failed to make any impression upon her sensitive mind. Vain she was not, and it would have been unjust to say that she was spoiled. She had a tender nature, full of sympathy for sorrow and suffering. She was constantly giving away her shoes, her stockings, nay, even her hood and cloak, to poor little invalids, whose misery appealed to her merciful heart. It was of no use to scold her; you could no more prevent a stream from flowing than Carina from giving. It was a spontaneous yielding to an impulse that was too strong to be resisted.

But to her father there was something unnatural in it; he would have preferred to have her frankly selfish, as most children are, not because he thought it lovely, but because it was childish and natural. Her unusual goodness gave him a pang more painful than ever the bad behavior of her brothers had occasioned. On the other hand, it delighted him to see her do anything that ordinary children did. He was charmed if she could be induced to take part in a noisy romp, play tag, or dress her dolls. But there followed usually after each outbreak of natural mirth a shy withdrawal into herself, a resolute and quiet retirement, as if she, were a trifle ashamed of her gayety. There was nothing morbid in these moods, no brooding sadness or repentance, but a touching solemnity, a serene, almost cheerful seriousness, which in one of her years seemed strange.

Mr. Holt had many a struggle with himself as to how he should treat Carina's delusion; and he made up his mind, at last, that it was his duty to do everything in his power to dispel and counteract it. When he happened to overhear her talking to her dolls one day, laying her hands upon them, and curing them of imaginary diseases, he concluded it was high time for him to act.

He called Carina to him, remonstrated kindly with her, and forbade her henceforth to see the people who came to her for the purpose of being cured. But it distressed him greatly to see how reluctantly she consented to obey him.

When Carina awoke the morning after this promise had been extorted from her, she heard the dogs barking furiously in the yard below. Her elder sister, Agnes, was standing half dressed before the mirror, holding the end of one blond braid between her teeth, while tying the other with a pink ribbon. Seeing that Carina was awake, she gave her a nod in the glass, and, removing her braid, observed that there evidently were sick pilgrims under the window. She could sympathize with Sultan and Hector, she averred, in their dislike of pilgrims.

"Oh, I wish they would not come! " sighed Carina. "It will be so hard for me to send them away. "

"I thought you liked curing people, " exclaimed Agnes.

"I do, sister, but papa has made me promise never to do it again. "

She arose and began to dress, her sister assisting her, chatting all the while like a gay little chirruping bird that neither gets nor expects an answer. She was too accustomed to Carina's moods to be either annoyed or astonished; but she loved her all the same, and knew that her little ears were wide open, even though she gave no sign of listening.

Carina had just completed her simple toilet when Guro, the chamber-maid, entered, and announced that there were some sick folk below who wished to see the wonder child.

"Tell them I cannot see them, " answered Carina, with a tremulous voice; "papa does not permit me. "

"But this man, Atle Pilot, has come from so far away in this dreadful cold, " pleaded Guro, "and his son is so very bad, poor thing; he's lying down in the boat, and he sighs and groans fit to move a stone."

"Don't! Don't tell her that, " interposed Agnes, motioning to the girl to begone. "Don't you see it is hard enough for her already? "

There was something in the air, as the two sisters descended the stairs hand in hand, which foreboded calamity. The pastor had given out from the pulpit last Sunday that he would positively receive no invalids at his house; and he had solemnly charged every one to refrain from bringing their sick to his daughter. He had repeated this announcement again and again, and he was now very much annoyed at his apparent powerlessness to protect his child from further imposition. Loud and angry speech was heard in his office, and a noise as if the furniture were being knocked about. The two little girls remained standing on the stairs, each gazing at the other's frightened face. Then there was a great bang, and a stalwart, elderly sailor came tumbling head foremost out into the hall. His cap was flung after him through the crack of the door. Agnes saw for an instant her father's face, red and excited; and in his bearing there was something wild and strange, which was so different from his usual gentle and dignified appearance. The sailor stood for a while bewildered, leaning against the wall; then he stooped slowly and picked up his cap. But the moment he caught sight of Carina his embarrassment vanished, and his rough features were illuminated with an intense emotion.

"Come, little miss, and help me, " he cried, in a hoarse, imploring whisper. "Halvor, my son—he is the only one God gave me—he is sick; he is going to die, miss, unless you take pity on him. "

"Where is he? " asked Carina.

"He's down in the boat, miss, at the pier. But I'll carry him up to you, if you like. We have been rowing half the night in the cold, and he is very low. "

"No, no; you mustn't bring him here, " said Agnes, seeing by Carina's face that she was on the point of yielding. "Father would be so angry. "

"He may kill me if he likes, " exclaimed the sailor, wildly. "It doesn't matter to me. But Halvor he's the only one I have, miss, and his mother died when he was born, and he is young, miss, and he will have many years to live, if you'll only have mercy on him. "

"But, you know, I shouldn't dare, on papa's account, to have you bring him here, " began Carina, struggling with her tears.

"Ah, yes! Then you will go to him. God bless you for that! " cried the poor man, with agonized eagerness. And interpreting the assent he read in Carina's eye, he caught her up in his arms, snatched a coat from a peg in the wall, and wrapping her in it, tore open the door. Carina made no outcry, and was not in the least afraid. She felt herself resting in two strong arms, warmly wrapped and borne away at a great speed over the snow. But Agnes, seeing her sister vanish in that sudden fashion, gave a scream which called her father to the door.

"What has happened? " he asked. "Where is Carina? "

"That dreadful Atle Pilot took her and ran away with her. "

"Ran away with her? " cried the pastor in alarm. "How? Where? "

"Down to the pier. "

It was a few moments' work for the terrified father to burst open the door, and with his velvet skull-cap on his head, and the skirts of his dressing-gown flying wildly about him, rush down toward the beach. He saw Atle Pilot scarcely fifty feet in advance of him, and shouted to him at the top of his voice. But the sailor only redoubled his speed, and darted out upon the pier, hugging tightly to his breast the precious burden he carried. So blindly did he rush ahead that the pastor expected to see him plunge headlong into the icy waves. But, as by a miracle, he suddenly checked himself, and grasping with one

51

hand the flag-pole, swung around it, a foot or two above the black water, and regained his foothold upon the planks. He stood for an instant irresolute, staring down into a boat which lay moored to the end of the pier. What he saw resembled a big bundle, consisting of a sheepskin coat and a couple of horse blankets.

"Halvor, " he cried, with a voice that shook with emotion, "I have brought her. "

There was presently a vague movement under the horse-blankets, and after a minute's struggle a pale yellowish face became visible. It was a young face—the face of a boy of fifteen or sixteen. But, oh, what suffering was depicted in those sunken eyes, those bloodless, cracked lips, and the shrunken yellow skin which clung in premature wrinkles about the emaciated features! An old and worn fur cap was pulled down over his ears, but from under its rim a few strands of blond hair were hanging upon his forehead.

Atle had just disentangled Carina from her wrappings, and was about to descend the stairs to the water when a heavy hand seized him by the shoulder, and a panting voice shouted in his ear:

"Give me back my child. "

He paused, and turned his pathetically bewildered face toward the pastor. "You wouldn't take him from me, parson, " he stammered, helplessly; "no, you wouldn't. He's the only one I've got. "

"I don't take him from you, " the parson thundered, wrathfully. "But what right have you to come and steal my child, because yours is ill?"

"When life is at stake, parson, " said the pilot, imploringly, "one gets muddled about right and wrong. I'll do your little girl no harm. Only let her lay her blessed hands upon my poor boy's head, and he will be well. "

"I have told you no, man, and I must put a stop to this stupid idolatry, which will ruin my child, and do you no good. Give her back to me, I say, at once. "

The pastor held out his hand to receive Carina, who stared at him with large pleading eyes out of the grizzly wolf-skin coat.

"Be good to him, papa, " she begged. "Only this once. "

"No, child; no parleying now; come instantly. "

And he seized her by main force, and tore her out of the pilot's arms. But to his dying day he remembered the figure of the heart-broken man, as he stood outlined against the dark horizon, shaking his clinched fists against the sky, and crying out, in a voice of despair:

"May God show you the same mercy on the Judgment Day as you have shown to me! "

II.

Six miserable days passed. The weather was stormy, and tidings of shipwreck and calamity filled the air. Scarcely a visitor came to the parsonage who had not some tale of woe to relate. The pastor, who was usually so gentle and cheerful, wore a dismal face, and it was easy to see that something was weighing on his mind.

"May God show you the same mercy on the Judgment Day as you have shown to me! "

These words rang constantly in his ears by night and by day. Had he not been right, according to the laws of God and man, in defending his household against the assaults of ignorance and superstition? Would he have been justified in sacrificing his own child, even if he could thereby save another's? And, moreover, was it not all a wild, heathenish delusion, which it was his duty as a servant of God to stamp out and root out at all hazards? Yes, there could be no doubt of it; he had but exercised his legal right. He had done what was demanded of him by laws human and divine. He had nothing to reproach himself for. And yet, with a haunting persistency, the image of the despairing pilot praying God for vengeance stared at him from every dark corner, and in the very church bells, as they rang out their solemn invitation to the house of God, he seemed to hear the rhythm and cadence of the heart-broken father's imprecation. In the depth of his heart there was a still small voice which told him that, say what he might, he had acted cruelly. If he put himself in Atle Pilot's place, bound as he was in the iron bonds of superstition, how different the case would look! He saw himself, in spirit, rowing in a lonely boat through the stormy winter night to his pastor, bringing his only son, who was at the point of death, and praying that the pastor's daughter might lay her hands upon him, as Christ had done to the blind, the halt, and the maimed. And his pastor received him with wrath, nay, with blows, and sent him away uncomforted. It was a hideous picture indeed, and Mr. Holt would have given years of his life to be rid of it.

It was on the sixth day after Atle's visit that the pastor, sitting alone in his study, called Carina to him. He had scarcely seen her during the last six days, or at least talked with her. Her sweet innocent spirit would banish the shadows that darkened his soul.

"Carina, " he said, in his old affectionate way, "papa wants to see you. Come here and let me talk a little with you. "

But could he trust his eyes? Carina, who formerly had run so eagerly into his arms, stood hesitating, as if she hoped to be excused.

"Well, my little girl, " he asked, in a tone of apprehension, "don't you want to talk with papa? "

"I would rather wait till some other time, papa, " she managed to stammer, while her little face flushed with embarrassment.

Mr. Holt closed the door silently, flung himself into a chair, and groaned. That was a blow from where he had least expected it. The child had judged him and found him wanting. His Carina, his darling, who had always been closest to his heart, no longer responded to his affection! Was the pilot's prayer being fulfilled? Was he losing his own child in return for the one he had refused to save? With a pang in his breast, which was like an aching wound, he walked up and down on the floor and marvelled at his own blindness. He had erred indeed; and there was no hope that any chance would come to him to remedy the wrong.

The twilight had deepened into darkness while he revolved this trouble in his mind. The night was stormy, and the limbs of the trees without were continually knocking and bumping against the walls of the house. The rusty weather-vane on the roof whined and screamed, and every now and then the sleet dashed against the window-panes like a handful of shot. The wind hurled itself against the walls, so that the timbers creaked and pulled at the shutters, banged stray doors in out-of-the-way garrets, and then, having accomplished its work, whirled away over the fields with a wild and dismal howl. The pastor sat listening mournfully to this tempestuous commotion. Once he thought he heard a noise as of a door opening near by him, and softly closing; but as he saw no one, he concluded it was his overwrought fancy that had played him a trick. He seated himself again in his easy-chair before the stove, which spread a dim light from its draught-hole into the surrounding gloom.

While he sat thus absorbed in his meditations, he was startled at the sound of something resembling a sob. He arose to strike a light, but found that his match-safe was empty. But what was that? A step without, surely, and the groping of hands for the door-knob.

"Who is there? " cried the pastor, with a shivering uneasiness.

He sprang forward and opened the door. A broad figure, surmounted by a sou'wester, loomed up in the dark.

"What do you want? " asked Mr. Holt, with forced calmness.

"I want to know, " answered a gruff, hoarse voice, "if you'll come to my son now, and help him into eternity? "

The pastor recognized Atle Pilot's voice, though it seemed harsher and hoarser than usual.

"Sail across the fjord on a night like this? " he exclaimed.

"That's what I ask you. "

"And the boy is dying, you say? "

"Can't last till morning. "

"And has he asked for the sacrament? "

The pilot stepped across the threshold and entered the room. He proceeded slowly to pull off his mittens; then looking up at the pastor's face, upon which a vague sheen fell from the stove, he broke out:

"Will you come or will you not? You wouldn't help him to live; now will you help him to die? "

The words, thrust forth with a slow, panting emphasis, hit the pastor like so many blows.

"I will come, " he said, with solemn resolution. "Sit down till I get ready. "

He had expected some expression of gratification or thanks, for Atle well knew what he had asked. It was his life the pastor risked, but this time in his calling as a physician, not of bodies, but of souls. It struck him, while he took leave of his wife, that there was something resentful and desperate in the pilot's manner, so different from his humble pleading at their last meeting.

As he embraced the children one by one, and kissed them, he missed Carina, but was told that she had probably gone to the cow-stable with the dairy-maid, who was her particular friend. So he left tender messages for her, and, summoning Atle, plunged out into the storm. A servant walked before him with a lantern, and lighted the way down to the pier, where the boat lay tossing upon the waves.

"But, man, " cried the pastor, seeing that the boat was empty, "where are your boatmen? "

"I am my own boatman, " answered Atle, gloomily. "You can hold the sheet, I the tiller. "

Mr. Holt was ashamed of retiring now, when he had given his word.

But it was with a sinking heart that he stepped into the frail skiff, which seemed scarcely more than a nutshell upon the tempestuous deep. He was on the point of asking his servant, unacquainted though he was with seamanship, to be the third man in the boat; but the latter, anticipating his intention, had made haste to betake himself away. To venture out into this roaring darkness, with no beacon to guide them, and scarcely a landmark discernible, was indeed to tempt Providence.

But by the time he had finished this reflection, the pastor felt himself rushing along at a tremendous speed, and short, sharp commands rang in his ears, which instantly engrossed all his attention. To his eyes the sky looked black as ink, except for a dark-blue unearthly shimmer that now and then flared up from the north, trembled, and vanished. By this unsteady illumination it was possible to catch a momentary glimpse of a head, and a peak, and the outline of a mountain. The small sail was double-reefed, yet the boat careened so heavily that the water broke over the gunwale. The squalls beat down upon them with tumultuous roar and smoke, as of snow-drifts, in their wake; but the little boat, climbing the top of the waves and sinking into the dizzy black pits between them, sped fearlessly along and the pastor began to take heart. Then, with a fierce cutting distinctness, came the command out of the dark.

"Pull out the reefs! "

"Are you crazy, man? " shouted the pastor. "Do you want to sail straight into eternity? "

"Pull out the reefs! " The command was repeated with wrathful emphasis.

"Then we are dead men, both you and I. "

"So we are, parson—dead men. My son lies dead at home, though you might have saved him. So, now, parson, we are quits. "

With a fierce laugh he rose up, and still holding the tiller, stretched his hand to tear out the reefs. But at that instant, just as a quivering shimmer broke across the sky, something rose up from under the thwart and stood between them. Atle started back with a hoarse scream.

"In Heaven's name, child! " he cried. "Oh, God, have mercy upon me! "

And the pastor, not knowing whether he saw a child or a vision, cried out in the same moment: "Carina, my darling! Carina, how came you here? "

It was Carina, indeed; but the storm whirled her tiny voice away over the waves, and her father, folding her with one arm to his breast, while holding the sheet with the other, did not hear what she answered to his fervent exclamation. He only knew that her dear little head rested close to his heart, and that her yellow hair blew across his face.

"I wanted to save that poor boy, papa, " were the only words that met his ears. But he needed no more to explain the mystery. It was Carina, who, repenting of her unkindness to him, had stolen into his study, while he sat in the dark, and there she had heard Atle Pilot's message. Even if this boy was sick unto death, she might perhaps cure him, and make up for her father's harshness. Thus reasoned the sage Carina; and she had gone secretly and prepared for the voyage, and battled with the storm, which again and again threw her down on her road to the pier. It was a miracle that she got safely into the boat, and stowed herself away snugly under the stern thwart.

The clearing in the north gradually spread over the sky, and the storm abated. Soon they had the shore in view, and the lights of the fishermen's cottages gleamed along the beach of the headland. Presently they ran into smoother water; a star or two flashed forth, and wide blue expanses appeared here and there on the vault of the sky. They spied the red lanterns marking the wharf, about which a multitude of boats lay, moored to stakes, and with three skilful tacks Atle made the harbor. It was here, standing on the pier, amid the swash and swirl of surging waters, that the pilot seized Carina's tiny hand in his big and rough one.

"Parson, " he said, with a breaking voice, "I was going to run afoul of you, and wreck myself with you; but this child, God bless her! she ran us both into port, safe and sound. "

But Carina did not hear what he said, for she lay sweetly sleeping in her father's arms.

"THE SONS OF THE VIKINGS"
I.

When Hakon Vang said his prayers at night, he usually finished with these words: "And I thank thee, God, most of all, because thou madest me a Norseman, and not a German or an Englishman or a Swede. "

To be a Norseman appears to the Norse boy a claim to distinction.

God has made so many millions of Englishmen and Russians and Germans, that there can be no particular honor in being one of so vast a herd; while of Norsemen He has made only a small and select number, whom He looks after with special care; upon whom He showers such favors as poverty and cold (with a view to keeping them good and hardy), and remoteness from all the glittering temptations that beset the nations in whom He takes a less paternal interest. Thus at least reasons, in a dim way, the small boy in Norway; thus he is taught to reason by his parents and instructors.

As for Hakon Vang, he strutted along the beach like a turkey-cock, whenever he thought of his glorious descent from the Vikings— those daring pirates that stole thrones and kingdoms, and mixed their red Norse blood in the veins of all the royal families of Europe. The teacher of history (who was what is called a Norse-Norseman) had on one occasion, with more patriotic zeal than discretion, undertaken to pick out those boys in his class who were of pure Norse descent; whose blood was untainted by any foreign admixture. The delighted pride of this small band made them an object of envy to all the rest of the school. Hakon, when his name was mentioned, felt as if he had added a yard to his height. Tears of joy started to his eyes; and to give vent to his overcharged feelings, he broke into a war-whoop; for which he received five black marks and was kept in at recess.

But he minded that very little; all great men, he reflected, have had to suffer for their country.

What Hakon loved above all things to study—nay, the only thing he loved to study—was the old Sagas, which are tales, poems, and histories of the deeds of the Norsemen in ancient times. With eleven of his classmates, who were about his own age and as Norse as himself, he formed a brotherhood which was called "The Sons of the Vikings. " They gave each other tremendously bloody surnames, in the style of the Sagas—names that reeked with gore and heroism. Hakon himself assumed the pleasing appellation "Skull-splitter, " and his classmate Frithjof Ronning was dubbed Vargr-i-Veum, which means Wolf-in-the-Temple. One Son of the Vikings was known as Ironbeard, another as Erling the Lop-Sided, a third as Thore the Hound, a fourth as Aslak Stone-Skull. But a serious difficulty, which came near disrupting the brotherhood, arose over these very names. It was felt that Hakon had taken an unfair advantage of the rest in selecting the bloodiest name at the outset (before anyone else had had an opportunity to choose), and there was a general demand that he should give it up and allow all to draw lots for it. But this Hakon stoutly refused to do; and declared that if anyone wanted his name he would have to fight for it, in good old Norse fashion.

A holm-gang or duel was then arranged; that is, a ring was marked out with stones; the combatants stepped within it, and he who could drive his antagonist outside of the stone ring was declared to be the victor. Frithjof, who felt that he had a better claim to be named Skull-Splitter than Hakon, was the first to accept the challenge; but after a terrible combat was forced to bite the dust. His conqueror was, however, filled with such a glowing admiration of his valor (as combatants in the Sagas frequently are), that he proposed that they should swear eternal friendship and foster-brotherhood, and seal their compact, according to Norse custom, by the ceremony called "Mingling of Blood. " It is needless to say that this seemed to all the boys a most delightful proposition; and they entered upon the august rite with a deep sense of its solemnity.

First a piece of sod, about twelve feet square, was carefully raised upon wooden stakes representing spears, so as to form a green roof over the foster-brothers. Then, sitting upon the black earth, where the turf had been removed, they bared their arms to the shoulder, and in the presence of his ten brethren, as witnesses, each swore that he would regard the other as his true brother and love him and treat him as such, and avenge his death if he survived him; in solemn testimony of which each drew a knife and opened a vein in his arm, letting their blood mingle and flow together. Hakon, however, in his heroic zeal, drove the knife into his flesh rather recklessly, and when the blood had flowed profusely for five minutes, he grew a trifle uneasy. Frithjof, after having bathed his arm in a neighboring brook, had no difficulty in stanching the blood, but the poor Skull-Splitter's wound, in spite of cold water and bandages, kept pouring forth its warm current without sign of abatement. Hakon grew paler and paler, and would have burst into tears, if he had not been a "Son of the Vikings. " It would have been a relief to him, for the moment, not to have been a "Son of the Vikings. " For he was terribly frightened, and thought surely he was going to bleed to death. The other Vikings, too, began to feel rather alarmed at such a prospect; and when Erling the Lop-Sided (the pastor's son) proposed that they should carry Hakon to the doctor, no one made any objection. But the doctor unhappily lived so far away that Hakon might die before he got there.

"Well, then, " said Wolf-in-the Temple, "let us take him to old Witch-Martha. She can stanch blood and do lots of other queer things. "

"Yes, and that is much more Norse, too, " suggested Thore the Hound; "wise women learned physic and bandaged wounds in the olden time. Men were never doctors. "

"Yes, Witch-Martha is just the right style, " said Erling the Lop-Sided down in his boots; for he had naturally a shrill voice and gave himself great pains to produce a manly bass.

"We must make a litter to carry the Skull-Splitter on, " exclaimed Einar Bowstring-Twanger (the sheriff's son); "he'll never get to Witch-Martha alive if he is to walk. "

This suggestion was favorably received, the boys set to work with a will, and in a few minutes had put together a litter of green twigs and branches. Hakon, who was feeling curiously light-headed and exhausted, allowed himself to be placed upon it in a reclining position; and its swinging motion, as his friends carried it along, nearly rocked him to sleep. The fear of death was but vaguely present to his mind; but his self-importance grew with every moment, as he saw his blood trickle through the leaves and drop at the roadside. He appeared to himself a brave Norse warrior who was being carried by his comrades from the battle-field, where he had greatly distinguished himself. And now to be going, to the witch who, by magic rhymes and incantations, was to stanch the ebbing stream of his life — what could be more delightful?

II.

Witch Martha lived in a small lonely cottage down by the river. Very few people ever went to see her in the day-time; but at night she often had visitors. Mothers who suspected that their children were changelings, whom the Trolds had put in the cradle, taking the human infants away; girls who wanted to "turn the hearts" of their lovers, and lovers who wanted to turn the hearts of the girls; peasants who had lost money or valuables and wanted help to trace the thief—these and many others sought secret counsel with Witch-Martha, and rarely went away uncomforted. She was an old weather-beaten woman with a deeply wrinkled, smoky-brown face, and small shrewd black eyes. The floor in her cottage was strewn with sand and fresh juniper twigs; from the rafters under the ceiling hung bunches of strange herbs; and in the windows were flower-pots with blooming plants in them.

Martha was stooping at the hearth, blowing and puffing at the fire under her coffee-pot, when the Sons of the Vikings knocked at the door. Wolf-in-the-Temple was the man who took the lead; and when Witch-Martha opened the upper half of the door (she never opened both at the same time) she was not a little astonished to see the Captain's son, Frithjof Ronning, staring up at her with an anxious face.

"What cost thou want, lad? " she asked, gruffly; "thou hast gone astray surely, and I'll show thee the way home. "

"I am Wolf-in-the-Temple, " began Frithjof, thrusting out his chest, and raising his head proudly.

"Dear me, you don't say so! " exclaimed Martha.

"My comrade and foster-brother Skull-Splitter has been wounded; and I want thee, old crone, to stanch his blood before he bleeds to death. "

"Dear, dear me, how very strange! " ejaculated the Witch, and shook her aged head.

She had been accustomed to extraordinary requests; but the language of this boy struck her as being something of the queerest she had yet heard.

"Where is thy Skull-Splitter, lad? " she asked, looking at him dubiously.

"Right here in the underbrush, " Wolf-in-the-Temple retorted, gallantly; "stir thy aged stumps now, and thou shalt be right royally rewarded. "

He had learned from Walter Scott's romances that this was the proper way to address inferiors, and he prided himself not a little on his jaunty condescension. Imagine then his surprise when the "old crone" suddenly turned on him with an angry scowl and said:

"If thou canst not keep a civil tongue in thy head, I'll bring a thousand plagues upon thee, thou umnannerly boy. "

By this threat Wolf-in-the-Temple's courage was sadly shaken. He knew Martha's reputation as a witch, and had no desire to test in his own person whether rumor belied her.

"Please, mum, I beg of you, " he said, with a sudden change of tone; "my friend Hakon Vang is bleeding to death; won't you please help him? "

"Thy friend Hakon Vang! " cried Martha, to whom that name was very familiar; "bring him in, as quick as thou canst, and I'll do what I can for him. "

Wolf-in- the-Temple put two fingers into his mouth and gave a loud shrill whistle, which was answered from the woods, and presently the small procession moved up to the door, carrying their wounded comrade between them. The poor Skull-Splitter was now as white as a sheet, and the drowsiness of his eyes and the laxness of his features showed that help came none too early. Martha, in hot haste, grabbed a bag of herbs, thrust it into a pot of warm water, and clapped it on the wound. Then she began to wag her head slowly to and fro, and crooned, to a soft and plaintive tune, words which sounded to the ears of the boys shudderingly strange:

"I conjure in water, I conjure in lead,
I conjure with herbs that grew o'er the dead;
I conjure with flowers that I plucked, without shoon,
When the ghosts were abroad, in the wane of the moon.
I conjure with spirits of earth and air
That make the wind sigh and cry in despair;
I conjure by him within sevenfold rings
That sits and broods at the roots of things.
I conjure by him who healeth strife,
Who plants and waters the germs of life.
I conjure, I conjure, I bid thee be still,
Thou ruddy stream, thou hast flowed thy fill!
Return to thy channel and nurture his life
Till his destined measure of years be rife. "

She sang the last two lines with sudden energy; and when she removed her hand from the wound, the blood had ceased to flow. The poor Skull-Splitter was sleeping soundly; and his friends, shivering a little with mysterious fears, marched up and down whispering to one another. They set a guard of honor at the leafy couch of their wounded comrade; intercepted the green worms and other insects that kept dropping down upon him from the alder branches overhead, and brushed away the flies that would fain disturb his slumbers. They were all steeped to the core in old Norse heroism; and they enjoyed the situation hugely. All the life about them was half blotted out; they saw it but dimly. That light of youthful romance, which never was on sea or land, transformed all the common things that met their vision into something strange and wonderful. They strained their ears to catch the meaning of the song of the birds, so that they might learn from them the secrets of the future, as Sigurd the Volsung did, after he had slain the dragon, Fafnir. The woods round about them were filled with dragons and fabulous beasts, whose tracks they detected with the eyes of faith; and they started out every morning, during the all too brief vacation, on imaginary expeditions against imaginary monsters.

When at the end of an hour the Skull-Splitter woke from his slumber, much refreshed, Witch-Martha bandaged his arm carefully, and Wolf-in-the Temple (having no golden arm-rings) tossed her, with magnificent superciliousness, his purse, which contained six cents. But she flung it back at him with such force that he had to dodge with more adroitness than dignity.

"I'll get my claws into thee some day, thou foolish lad, " she said, lifting her lean vulture-like hand with a threatening gesture.

"No, please don't, Martha, I didn't mean anything, " cried the boy, in great alarm; "you'll forgive me, won't you, Martha? "

"I'll bid thee begone, and take thy foolish tongue along with thee, " she answered, in a mollified tone.

And the Sons of the Vikings, taking the hint, shouldered the litter once more, and reached Skull-Splitter's home in time for supper.

III.

The Sons of the Vikings were much troubled. Every heroic deed which they plotted had this little disadvantage, that they were in danger of going to jail for it. They could not steal cattle and horses, because they did not know what to do with them when they had got them; they could not sail away over the briny deep in search of fortune or glory, because they had no ships; and sail-boats were scarcely big enough for daring voyages to the blooming South which their ancestors had ravaged. The precious vacation was slipping away, and as yet they had accomplished nothing that could at all be called heroic. It was while the brotherhood was lamenting this fact that Wolf-in-the-Temple had a brilliant idea. He procured his father's permission to invite his eleven companions to spend a day and a night at the Ronning saeter, or mountain dairy, far up in the highlands. The only condition Mr. Ronning made was that they were to be accompanied by his man, Brumle-Knute, who was to be responsible for their safety. But the boys determined privately to make Brumle-Knute their prisoner, in case he showed any disposition to spoil their sport. To spend a day and a night in the woods, to imagine themselves Vikings, and behave as they imagined Vikings would behave, was a prospect which no one could contemplate without the most delightful excitement. There, far away from sheriffs and pastors and maternal supervision, they might perhaps find the long-desired chance of performing their heroic deed.

It was a beautiful morning early in August that the boys started from Strandholm, Mr. Ronning's estate, accompanied by Brumle-Knute. The latter was a middle-aged, round-shouldered peasant, who had the habit of always talking to himself. To look at him you would have supposed that he was a rough and stupid fellow who would have quite enough to do in looking after himself. But the fact was, that Brumle-Knute was the best shot, the best climber—and altogether the most keen-eyed hunter in the whole valley. It was a saying that he could scent game so well that he never needed a dog; and that he could imitate to perfection the call of every game bird that inhabited the mountain glens. Sweet-tempered he was not; but so reliable, skilful, and vigilant, and moreover so thorough a woodsman, that the boys could well afford to put up with his gruff temper.

The Sons of the Vikings were all mounted on ponies; and Wolf-in-the-Temple, who had been elected chieftain, led the troop. At his side rode Skull-Splitter, who was yet a trifle pale after his blood-letting, but brimming over with ambition to distinguish himself. They had all tied their trousers to their legs with leather thongs, in order to be perfectly "Old Norse; " and some of them had turned their plaids and summer overcoats inside out, displaying the gorgeous colors of the lining. Loosely attached about their necks and flying in the wind, these could easily serve for scarlet or purple cloaks wrought on Syrian looms. Most of the boys carried also wooden swords and shields, and the chief had a long loor or Alpine horn. Only the valiant Ironbeard, whose father was a military man, had a real sword and a real scabbard into the bargain. Wolf-in-the-Temple, and Erling the Lop-Sided, had each an old fowling-piece; and Brumle-Knute carried a double-barrelled rifle. This, to be sure, was not; quite historically correct; but firearms are so useful in the woods, even if they are not correct, that it was resolved not to notice the irregularity; for there were boars in the mountains, besides wolves and foxes and no end of smaller game.

For an hour or more the procession rode, single file, up the steep and rugged mountain-paths; but the boys were all in high spirits and enjoyed themselves hugely. The mere fact that they were Vikings, on a daring foraging expedition into a neighboring kingdom, imparted a wonderful zest to everything they did and said. It might be foolish, but it was on that account none the less delightful. They sent out scouts to watch for the approach of an imaginary enemy; they had secret pass-words and signs; they swore (Viking style) by Thor's hammer and by Odin's eye. They talked appalling nonsense to each other with a delicious sentiment of its awful blood-curdling character. It was about noon when they reached the Strandholm saeter, which consisted of three turf-thatched log-cabins or chalets, surrounded by a green inclosure of half a dozen acres. The wide highland plain, eight or ten miles long, was bounded on the north and west by throngs of snow-hooded mountain peaks, which rose, one behind another, in glittering grandeur; and in the middle of the plain there were two lakes or tarns, connected by a river which was milky white where it entered the lakes and clear as crystal where it escaped.

"Now, Vikings, " cried Wolf-in-the-Temple, when the boys had done justice to their dinner, "it behooves us to do valiant deeds, and to prove ourselves worthy of our fathers. "

"Hear, hear, " shouted Ironbeard, who was fourteen years old and had a shadow of a moustache, "I am in for great deeds, hip, hip, hurrah! "

"Hold your tongue when you hear me speak, " commanded the chieftain, loftily; "we will lie in wait at the ford, between the two tarns, and capture the travellers who pass that way. If perchance a princess from the neighboring kingdom pass, on the way to her dominions, we will hold her captive until her father, the king, comes to ransom her with heaps of gold in rings and fine garments and precious weapons. "

"But what are we to do with her when we have caught her? " asked the Skull-Splitter, innocently.

"We will keep her imprisoned in the empty saeter hut, " Wolf-in-the-Temple responded. "Now, are you ready? We'll leave the horses here on the croft, until our return. "

The question now was to elude Brumle-Knute's vigilance; for the Sons of the Vikings had good reasons for fearing that he might interfere with their enterprise. They therefore waited until Brumle-knute was invited by the dairymaid to sit down to dinner. No sooner had the door closed upon his stooping figure, than they stole out through a hole in the fence, crept on all-fours among the tangled dwarf-birches and the big gray boulders, and following close in the track of their leader, reached the ford between the lakes. There they observed two enormous heaps of stones known as the Parson and the Deacon; for it had been the custom from immemorial times for every traveller to fling a big stone as a "sacrifice" for good luck upon the Parson's heap and a small stone upon the Deacon's. Behind these piles of stone the boys hid themselves, keeping a watchful eye on the road and waiting for their chief's signal to pounce upon unwary travellers. They lay for about fifteen minutes in expectant silence, and were on the point of losing their patience.

"Look here, Wolf-in-the-Temple, " cried Erling the Lop-Sided, "you may think this is fun, but I don't. Let us take the raft there and go fishing. The tarn is simply crowded with perch and bass. "

"Hold your disrespectful tongue, " whispered the chief, warningly, "or I'll discipline you so you'll remember it till your dying day. "

"Ho, ho! " laughed the rebel, jeeringly; "big words and fat pork don't stick in the throat. Wait till I get you alone and we shall see who'll be disciplined. "

Erling had risen and was about to emerge from his hiding-place, when suddenly hoof-beats were heard, and a horse was seen approaching, carrying on its back a stalwart peasant lass, in whose lap a pretty little girl of twelve or thirteen was sitting.

The former was clad in scarlet bodice, a black embroidered skirt, and a snowy-white kerchief was tied about her head. Her blonde hair hung in golden profusion down over her back and shoulders. The little girl was city-clad, and had a sweet and appealing face. She was chattering guilelessly with her companion, asking more questions than she could possibly expect to have answered. Nearer and nearer they came to the great stone heaps, dreaming of no harm.

"And, Gunbjor, " the Skull-Splitter heard the little girl say, "you don't really believe that there are trolds and fairies in the mountains, do you? "

"Them as are wiser than I am have believed that, " was Gunbjor's answer; "but we don't hear so much about the trolds nowadays as they did when my granny was young. Then they took young girls into the mountain and — —"

Here came a wild, piercing yell, as the Sons of the Vikings rushed forward from behind the rocks, and with a terrible war-whoop swooped down upon the road. Wolf-in-the-Temple, who led the band, seized the horse by the bridle, and flourishing his sword threateningly, addressed the frightened peasant lass.

"Is this, perchance, the Princess Kunigunde, the heir to the throne of my good friend, King Bjorn the Victorious? " he asked, with a magnificent air, seizing the trembling little girl by the wrist.

"Nay, " Gunbjor answered, as soon as she could find her voice, "this is the Deacon's Maggie, as is going to the saeter with me to spend Sunday. "

"She cannot proceed on her way, " said the chieftain, decisively, "she is my prisoner. "

Gunbjor, who had been frightened out of her wits by the small red- and blue-cloaked men, swarming among the stones, taking them to be trolls or fairies, now gradually recovered her senses. She recognized in Erling the Lop-Sided the well-known features of the parson's son; and as soon as she had made this discovery she had no great difficulty in identifying the rest. "Never you fear, pet, " she said to the child in her lap, "these be bad boys as want to frighten us. I'll give them a switching if they don't look out. "

"The Princess Kunigunde is my prisoner until it please her noble father to ransom her for ten pounds of silver, " repeated Wolf-in-the-Temple, putting his arm about little Maggie's waist and trying to lift her from the saddle.

"You keep yer hands off the child, or I'll give you ten pounds of thrashing, " cried Gunbjor, angrily.

"She shall be treated with the respect due to her rank, " Wolf-in-the-Temple proceeded, loftily. "I give King Bjorn the Victorious three moons in which to bring me the ransom. "

"And I'll give you three boxes on the ear, and a cut with my whip, into the bargain, if you don't let the horse alone, and take yer hands off the child. "

"Vikings! " cried the chief, "lay hands on her! Tear her from the saddle! She has defied us! She deserves no mercy. "

With a tremendous yell the boys rushed forward, brandishing their swords above their heads, and pulled Gunbjor from the saddle. But she held on to her charge with a vigorous clutch, and as soon as her feet touched the ground she began with her disengaged hand to lay

69

about her, with her whip, in a way that proved extremely unpleasant. Wolf-in-the-Temple, against whom her assault was especially directed, received some bad cuts across his face, and Ironbeard was driven backward into the ford, where he fell, full length, and rose dripping wet and mortified. Thore the Hound got a thump in his head from Gunbjor's stalwart elbows, and Skull-Splitter, who had more courage than discretion, was pitched into the water with no more ceremony than if he had been a superfluous kitten. The fact was—I cannot disguise it—within five minutes the whole valiant band of the Sons of the Vikings were routed by that terrible switch, wielded by the intrepid Gunbjor. When the last of her foes had bitten the dust, she calmly remounted her pony, and with the Deacon's Maggie in her lap rode, at a leisurely pace, across the ford.

"Good-by, lads, " she said, nodding her head at them over her shoulder; "ye needn't be afraid. I won't tell on you. "

IV.

To have been routed by a woman was a terrible humiliation to the valiant Sons of the Vikings. They were silent and moody during the evening, and sat staring into the big bonfire on the saeter green with stern and melancholy features. They had suffered defeat in battle, and it behooved them to avenge it. About nine o'clock they retired into their bunks in the log cabin, but no sooner was Brumle-Knute's rhythmic snoring perceived than Wolf-in-the-Temple put his head out and called to his comrades to meet him in front of the house for a council of war. Instantly they scrambled out of their alcoves, pulled on their coats and trousers; and noiselessly stole out into the night. The sun was yet visible, but a red veil of fiery mist was drawn across his face; and a magic air of fairy-tales and strange unreality was diffused over mountains, plains and lakes. The river wound like a huge, blood-red serpent through the mountain pastures, and the snow-hooded peaks blazed with fiery splendor.

The boys were quite stunned at the sight of such magnificence, and stood for some minutes gazing at the landscape, before giving heed to the summons of the chief.

"Comrades, " said Wolf-in-the-Temple, solemnly, "what is life without honor? "

There was not a soul present who could answer that conundrum, and after a fitting pause the chief was forced to answer it himself.

"Life without honor, comrades, " he said, severely, "life—without honor is—nothing. "

"Hear, hear! " cried Ironbeard; "good for you, old man! "

"Silence! " thundered Wolf-in-the-Temple, "I must beg the gentlemen to observe the proprieties. "

This tremendous phrase rarely failed to restore order, and the flippant Ironbeard was duly rebuked by the glances of displeasure which met him on all sides. But in the meanwhile the chief had lost the thread of his speech and could not recover it. "Vikings, " he resumed, clearing his throat vehemently, "we have been—that is to say—we have sustained——"

"A thrashing, " supplied the innocent Skull-Splitter.

But the awful stare which was fixed upon him convinced him that he had made a mistake; and he shrunk into an abashed silence. "We must do something to retrieve our honor, " continued the chief, earnestly; "we must—take steps—to to get upon our legs again, " he finished, blushing with embarrassment.

"I would suggest that we get upon our legs first, and take the steps afterward, " remarked the flippant Ironbeard, with a sly wink at Thore the Hound.

The chief held it to be beneath his dignity to notice this interruption, and after having gazed for a while in silence at the blood-red mountain peaks, he continued, more at his ease:

"I propose, comrades, that we go on a bear hunt. Then, when we return with a bear-skin or two, our honor will be all right; no one will dare laugh at us. The brave boy-hunters will be the admiration and pride of the whole valley. "

"But Brummle-Knute, " observed the Skull-Splitter; "do you think he will allow us to go bear-hunting? "

"What do we care whether he allows us or not? " cried Wolf-in-the-Temple, scornfully; "he sleeps like a log; and I propose that we tie his hands and feet before we start. "

This suggestion met with enthusiastic approval, and all the boys laughed heartily at the idea of Brumle-Knute waking up and finding himself tied with ropes, like a calf that is carried to market.

"Now, comrades, " commanded the chief, with a flourish of his sword, "get to bed quickly. I'll call you at four o'clock; we'll then start to chase the monarch of the mountains. "

The Sons of the Vikings scrambled into their bunks with great despatch; and though their beds consisted of pine twigs, covered with a coarse sheet, and a bat, of straw for a pillow, they fell asleep without rocking, and slept more soundly than if they had rested on silken bolsters filled with eiderdown. Wolf-in-the-Temple was as good as his word, and waked them promptly at four o'clock; and their first task, after having filled their knapsacks with provisions, was to tie Brumle-Knute's hands and feet with the most cunning slip-knots, which would tighten more, the more he struggled to unloose them. Ironbeard, who had served a year before the mast, was the contriver of this daring enterprise; and he did it so cleverly that Brumle-Knute never suspected that his liberty was being interfered with. He snorted a little and rubbed imaginary cobwebs from his face; but soon lapsed again into a deep, snoring unconsciousness.

The faces of the Sons of the Vikings grew very serious as they started out on this dangerous expedition. There was more than one of them who would not have objected to remaining at home, but who feared to incur the charge of cowardice if he opposed the wishes of the rest. Wolf-in-the-Temple walked at the head of the column, as they hastened with stealthy tread out of the saeter inclosure, and steered their course toward the dense pine forest, the tops of which were visible toward the east, where the mountain sloped toward the valley. He carried his fowling-piece, loaded with shot, in his right hand, and a powder-horn and other equipments for the chase were flung across his shoulder. Erling the Lop-Sided was similarly armed, and Ironbeard, glorying in a real sword, unsheathed it every minute and let it flash in the sun. It was a great consolation to the rest of the Vikings to see these formidable weapons; for they were not wise enough to know that grown-up bears are not killed with shot, and that a fowling-piece is a good deal more dangerous than no weapon at all, in the hands of an inexperienced hunter.

The sun, who had exchanged his flaming robe de nuit for the rosy colors of morning, was now shooting his bright shafts of light across the mountain plain, and cheering the hearts of the Sons of the Vikings. The air was fresh and cool; and it seemed a luxury to breathe it. It entered the lungs in a pure, vivifying stream like an elixir of life, and sent the blood dancing through the veins. It was impossible to mope in such air; and Ironbeard interpreted the general mood when he struck up the tune:

"We wander with joy on the far mountain path, We follow the star that will guide us; "

but before he had finished the third verse, it occurred to the chief that they were bear-hunters, and that it was very unsportsmanlike behavior to sing on the chase. For all that they were all very jolly, throbbing with excitement at the thought of the adventures which they were about to encounter; and concealing a latent spark of fear under an excess of bravado. At the end of an hour's march they had reached the pine forest; and as they were all ravenously hungry they sat down upon the stones, where a clear mountain brook ran down the slope, and unpacked their provisions. Wolf-in-the-Temple had just helped himself, in old Norse fashion, to a slice of smoked ham, having slashed a piece off at random with his knife, when Erling the Lop-Sided observed that that ham had a very curious odor. Everyone had to test its smell; and they all agreed that it did have a singular flavor, though its taste was irreproachable.

"It smells like a menagerie, " said the Skull-Splitter, as he handed it to Thore the Hound.

"But the bread and the biscuit smell just the same, " said Thore the Hound; "in fact, it is the air that smells like a menagerie. "

"Boys, " cried Wolf-in-the-Temple, "do you see that track in the mud? "

"Yes; it is the track of a barefooted man, " suggested the innocent Skull-Splitter.

Ironbeard and Erling the Lop-Sided flung themselves down among the stones and investigated the tracks; and they were no longer in doubt as to where the pungent wild odor came from, which they had attributed to the ham.

"Boys, " said Erling, looking up with an excited face, "a she-bear with one or two cubs has been here within a few minutes. "

"This is her drinking-place, " said Ironbeard: "the tracks are many and well-worn; if she hasn't been here this morning, she is sure to come before long. "

"We are in luck indeed, " Wolf-in-the-Temple observed, coolly; "we needn't go far for our bear. He will be coming for us. "

At that moment the note of an Alpine horn was heard; but it was impossible to determine how far it was away; for the echo took up the note and flung it back and forth with clear and strong reverberations from mountain to mountain.

"It is Brumle-Knute who is calling us, " said Thore the Hound. "The dairymaid must have released him. Shall we answer? "

"Never, " cried the chief, proudly; "I forbid you to answer. Here we have our heroic deed in sight, and I want no one to spoil it. If there is a coward among us, let him take to his heels; no one shall detain him. "

There were perhaps several who would have liked to accept the invitation; but no one did. Skull-Splitter, by way of diversion, plumped backward into the brook, and sat down in the cool pool up to his waist. But nobody laughed at his mishap; because they had their minds full of more serious thoughts. Wolf-in-the-Temple, who had climbed up on a big moss-grown boulder, stood, gun in hand, and peered in among the bushes.

"Boys, " he whispered, "drop down on your bellies — quick. "

All, crowding behind a rock, obeyed, pushing themselves into position with hands and feet. With wildly beating hearts the Vikings gazed up among the gray wilderness of stone and underbrush, and first one, then another, caught sight of something brown and hairy that came toddling down toward them, now rolling like a ball of yarn, now turning a somersault, and now again pegging industriously along on four clumsy paws. It was the prettiest little bear cub that ever woke on its mossy lair in the woods. Now it came shuffling down in a boozy way to take its morning bath. It seemed but half awake; and Skull-Splitter imagined that it was a trifle cross, because its mother had waked it too early. Evidently it had made no toilet as yet, for bits of moss were sticking in its hair; and it yawned once or twice, and shook its head disgustedly. Skull-Splitter knew so well that feeling and could sympathize with the poor young cub. But Wolf-in-the-Temple, who watched it no less intently, was filled with quite different emotions. Here was his heroic deed, for which he had hungered so long. To shoot a bear—that was a deed worthy of a Norseman. One step more—then two—and then—up rose the bear cub on its hind legs and rubbed its eyes with its paws. Now he had a clean shot—now or never; and pulling the trigger Wolf-in-the-Temple blazed away and sent a handful of shot into the carcass of the poor little bear. Up jumped all the Sons of the Vikings from behind their stones, and, with a shout of triumph, ran up the path to where the cub was lying. It had rolled itself up into a brown ball, and whimpered like a child in pain. But at that very moment there came an ominous growl out of the underbrush, and a crackling and creaking of branches was heard which made the hearts of the boys stand still.

"Erling, " cried Wolf-in-the-Temple, "hand me your gun, and load mine for me as quick as you can. "

The words were scarcely out of his mouth when the head of a big brown she-bear became visible among the bushes. She paused in the path, where her cub was lying, turned him over with her paw, licked his face, grumbled with a low soothing tone, snuffed him all over and rubbed her nose against his snout. But unwarily she must have touched some sore spot; for the cub gave a sharp yelp of pain and writhed and whimpered as he looked up into his mother's eyes, clumsily returning her caresses. The boys, half emerged from their hiding-places, stood watching this demonstration of affection not without sympathy; and Skull-Splitter, for one, heartily wished that the chief had not wounded the little bear. Quite ignorant as he was of the nature of bears, he allowed his compassion to get the better of his judgment. It seemed such a pity that the poor little beast should lie there and suffer with one eye put out and forty or fifty bits of lead distributed through its body. It would be much more merciful to put it out of its misery altogether. And accordingly when Erling the Lop-

Sided handed him his gun to pass on to the chief, Skull-Splitter started forward, flung the gun to his cheek, and blazed away at the little bear once more, entirely heedless of consequences. It was a random, unskilful shot, which was about equally shared by the cub and its mother. And the latter was not in a mood to be trifled with. With an angry roar she rose on her hind legs and advanced against the unhappy Skull-Splitter with two uplifted paws. In another moment she would give him one of her vigorous "left-handers, " which would probably pacify him forever. Ironbeard gave a scream of terror and Thore the Hound broke down an alder-sapling in his excitement. But Wolf-in-the-Temple, remembering that he had sworn foster-brotherhood with this brave and foolish little lad, thought that now was the time to show his heroism. Here it was no longer play, but dead earnest. Down he leaped from his rock, and just as the she-bear was within a foot of the Skull-Splitter, he dealt her a blow in the head with the butt end of his gun which made the sparks dance before her eyes. She turned suddenly toward her new assailant, growling savagely, and scratched her ear with her paw. And Skull-Splitter, who had slipped on the pine needles and fallen, scrambled to his feet again, leaving his gun on the ground, and with a few aimless steps tumbled once more into the brook. Ironbeard, seeing that he was being outdone by his chief, was quick to seize the gun, and rushing forward dealt the she-bear another blow, which, instead of disabling her, only exasperated her further. She glared with her small bloodshot eyes now at the one, now at the other boy, as if in doubt which she would tackle first. It was an awful moment; one or the other might have saved himself by flight, but each was determined to stand his ground. Vikings could die, but never flee. With a furious growl the she-bear started toward her last assailant, lifting her terrible paw. Ironbeard backed a few steps, pointing his gun before him; and with benumbing force the paw descended upon the gun-barrel, striking it out of his hands.

It seemed all of a sudden to the boy as if his arms were asleep up to the shoulders; he had a stinging sensation in his flesh and a humming in his ears, which made him fear that his last hour had come. If the bear renewed the attack now, he was utterly defenceless. He was not exactly afraid, but he was numb all over. It seemed to matter little what became of him.

But now a strange thing happened. To his unutterable astonishment he saw the she-bear drop down on all fours and vent her rage on the gun, which, in a trice, was bent and broken into a dozen fragments.

But in this diversion she was interrupted by Wolf-in-the-Temple, who hammered away again at her head with the heavy end of his weapon. Again she rose, and presented two rows of white teeth which looked as if they meant business. It was the chief's turn now to meet his fate; and it was the more serious because his helper was disarmed and could give him no assistance. With a wildly thumping heart he raised the butt end of his gun and dashed forward, when as by a miracle a shot was heard—a sharp, loud shot that rumbled away with manifold reverberations among the mountains. In the same instant the huge brown bear tumbled forward, rolled over, with a gasping growl, and was dead.

"O Brumle-Knute! Brumle-Knute! " yelled the boys in joyous chorus, as they saw their resuer coming forward from behind the rocks, "how did you find us? "

"I heard yer shots and I saw yer tracks, " said Brumle-Knute, dryly; "but when ye go bear-hunting another time ye had better load with bullets instead of bird-shot. "

"But Brumle-Knute, we only wanted to shoot the little bear, " protested Wolf-in-the-Temple.

"That may be, " Brumle-Knute replied; "but the big bears, they are a curiously unreasonable lot—they are apt to get mad when you fire at their little ones. Next time you must recollect to take the big bear into account. "

I need not tell you that the Sons of the Vikings became great heroes when the rumor of their bear hunt was noised abroad through the valley. But, for all that, they determined to disband their brotherhood. Wolf-in-the-Temple expressed the sentiment of all when, at their last meeting, he made a speech, in which these words occurred:

"Brothers, the world isn't quite the same now as it was in the days when our Viking forefathers spread the terror of their name through the South. We are not so strong as they were, nor so hardy. When we mingle blood, we have to send for a surgeon. If we steal princesses we may go to jail for it—or—or—well—never mind—what else may happen. Heroism isn't appreciated as once it was in this country; and I, for one, won't try to be a hero any more. I resign my chieftainship now, when I can do it with credit. Let us all make our bows of adieu as bear hunters; and if we don't do anything more in the heroic line it is not because we can't, but because we won't. "

PAUL JESPERSEN'S MASQUERADE

There was great excitement in the little Norse town, Bumlebro, because there was going to be a masquerade. Everybody was busy inventing the character which he was to represent, and the costume in which he was to represent it.

Miss Amelia Norbeck, the apothecary's daughter, had intended to be Marie Antoinette, but had to give it up because the silk stockings were too dear, although she had already procured the beauty-patches and the powdered wig.

Miss Arctander, the judge's daughter, was to be Night, in black tulle, spangled with silver stars, and Miss Hanna Broby was to be Morning, in white tulle and pink roses.

There had never BEEN a masquerade in Bumlebro, and there would not have been one now, if it had not been for the enterprise of young Arctander and young Norbeck, who had just returned from the military academy in the capital, and were anxious to exhibit themselves to the young girls in their glory.

Of course, they could not afford to be exclusive, for there were but twenty or thirty families in the town that laid any claims to gentility, and they had all to be invited in order to fill the hall and pay the bills. Thus it came to pass that Paul Jespersen, the book-keeper in the fish-exporting firm of Broby & Larsen, received a card, although, to be sure, there had been a long debate in the committee as to where the line should be drawn.

Paul Jespersen was uncommonly elated when he read the invitation, which was written on a gilt-edged card, requesting the pleasure of Mr. Jespersen's company at a bal masque Tuesday, January 3d, in the Association Hall.

"The pleasure of his company! "

Think of it! He felt so flattered that he blushed to the tips of his ears. It must have been Miss Clara Broby who had induced them to be so polite to him, for those insolent cadets, who only nodded patronizingly to him in response to his deferential greeting, would never have asked for "the pleasure of his company. "

Having satisfied himself on this point, Paul went to call upon Miss Clara in the evening, in order to pay her some compliment and consult her in regard to his costume; but Miss Clara, as it happened, was much more interested in her own costume than in that of Mr. Jespersen, and offered no useful suggestions.

"What character would you advise me to select, Mr. Jespersen? " she inquired, sweetly. "My sister Hanna, you know, is going to be Morning, so I can't be that, and it seems to me Morning would have suited me just lovely. "

"Go as Beauty, " suggested Mr. Jespersen, blushing at the thought of his audacity.

"So I will, Mr. Jespersen, " she answered, laughing, "if you will go as the Beast. "

Paul, being a simple-hearted fellow, failed to see any sarcasm in this, but interpreted it rather as a hint that Miss Clara desired his escort, as Beauty, of course, only would be recognizable in her proper character by the presence of the Beast.

"I shall be delighted, Miss Clara, " he said, beaming with pleasure. "If you will be my Beauty, I'll be your Beast. "

Miss Clara did not know exactly how to take this, and was rather absent-minded during the rest of the interview. She had been chaffing Mr. Jespersen, of course, but she did not wish to be absolutely rude to him, because he was her father's employee, and, as she often heard her father say, a very valuable and trustworthy young man.

When Paul got home he began at once to ponder upon his character as Beast, and particularly as Miss Clara's Beast. It occurred to him that his uncle, the furrier, had an enormous bear-skin, with head, eyes, claws, and all that was necessary, and without delay he went to try it on.

His uncle, feeling that this event was somehow to redound to the credit of the family, agreed to make the necessary alterations at a trifling cost, and when the night of the masquerade arrived, Paul was so startled at his appearance that he would have run away from himself if such a thing had been possible. He had never imagined that he would make such a successful Beast.

By an ingenious contrivance with a string, which he pulled with his hand, he was able to move his lower jaw, which, with its red tongue and terrible teeth, presented an awful appearance. By patching the skin a little behind, his head was made to fit comfortably into the bear's head, and his mild blue eyes looked out of the holes from which the bear's eyes had been removed. The skin was laced with thin leather thongs from the neck down, but the long, shaggy fur made the lacing invisible.

Paul Jespersen practiced ursine behavior before the looking-glass for about half an hour. Then, being uncomfortably warm, he started down-stairs, and determined to walk to the Association Hall. He chuckled to himself at the thought of the sensation he would make, if he should happen to meet anybody on the road.

Having never attended a masquerade before, he did not know that dressing-rooms were provided for the maskers, and, being averse to needless expenditure, he would as soon have thought of flying as of taking a carriage. There was, in fact, but one carriage on runners in the town, and that was already engaged by half a dozen parties.

The moon was shining faintly upon the snow, and there was a sharp frost in the air when Paul Jespersen put his hairy head out of the street-door and reconnoitred the territory.

There was not a soul to be seen, except an old beggar woman who was hobbling along, supporting herself with two sticks. Paul darted, as quickly as his unwieldly bulk would allow, into the middle of the street. He enjoyed intensely the fun of walking abroad in such a monstrous guise. He contemplated with boyish satisfaction his shadow which stretched, long and black and horrible, across the snow.

It was a bit slippery, and he had to manoeuvre carefully in order to keep right side up. Presently he caught up with the beggar woman.

"Good-evening! " he said.

The old woman turned about, stared at him horror-stricken; then, as soon as she had collected her senses, took to her heels, yelling at the top of her voice. A big mastiff, who had just been let loose for the night, began to bark angrily in a back yard, and a dozen comrades responded from other yards, and came bounding into the street.

"Hello! " thought Paul Jespersen. "Now look out for trouble. "

He felt anything but hilarious when he saw the pack of angry dogs dancing and leaping about him, barking in a wildly discordant chorus.

"Why, Hector, you fool, don't you know me? " he said, coaxingly, to the judge's mastiff. "And you, Sultan, old man! You ought to be ashamed of yourself! Here, Caro, that's a good fellow! Come, now, don't excite yourself! "

But Hector, Sultan, and Caro were all proof against such blandishments, and as for Bismarck, the apothecary's collie, he grew every moment more furious, and showed his teeth in a very uncomfortable fashion.

To defend one's self was not to be thought of, for what defence is possible to a sham bear against a dozen genuine dogs? Paul could use neither his teeth nor his claws to any purpose, while the dogs could use theirs, as he presently discovered, with excellent effect.

He had just concluded to seek safety in flight, when suddenly he felt a bite in his left calf, and saw the brute Bismarck tug away at his leg as if it had been a mutton-chop. He had scarcely recovered from this surprise when he heard a sharp report, and a bullet whizzed away over his head, after having neatly put a hole through the right ear. Paul concluded, with reason, that things were getting serious.

If he could only get hold of that blockhead, the judge's groom, who was violating the law about fire-arms, he would give him an exhibition in athletics which he would not soon forget; but, being for the moment deprived of this pleasure, he knew of nothing better to do than to dodge through the nearest street-door, and implore the protection of the very first individual he might meet.

It so happened that Paul selected the house of two middle-aged milliners for this experiment.

Boyhood in Norway

Jemina and Malla Hansen were just seated at the table drinking tea with their one constant visitor, the post-office clerk, Mathias, when, all of a sudden, they heard a tremendous racket in the hall, and the furious barking of dogs.

With a scream of fright, the two old maids jumyed up, dropping their precious tea-cups, and old Mathias, who had tipped his chair a little backward, lost his balance, and pointed his heels toward the ceiling. Before he had time to pick himself up the door was burst open and a great hairy monster sprang into the room.

"Mercy upon us! " cried Jemina. "It is the devil! "

But now came the worst of it all. The bear put his paw on his heart, and with the politest bow in the world, remarked:

"Pardon me, ladies, if I intrude. "

He had meant to say more, but his audience had vanished; only the flying tails of Mathias's coat were seen, as he slammed the door on them, in his precipitate flight.

"Police! police! " someone shouted out of the window of the adjoining room.

Police! Now, with all due respect for the officers of the law, Paul Jespersen had no desire to meet them at the present moment. To be hauled up at the station-house and fined for street disorder—nay, perhaps be locked up for the night, if, as was more than likely, the captain of police was at the masquerade, was not at all to Paul's taste. Anything rather than that! He would be the laughing stock of the whole town if, after his elaborate efforts, he were to pass the night in a cell, instead of dancing with Miss Clara Broby.

Hearing the cry for police repeated, Paul looked about him for some means of escape. It occurred to him that he had seen a ladder in the hall leading up to the loft. There he could easily hide himself until the crowd had dispersed.

Without further reflection, he rushed out through the door by which he had entered, climbed the ladder, thrust open a trap-door, and, to his astonishment, found himself under the wintry sky.

The roof sloped steeply, and he had to balance carefully in order to avoid sliding down into the midst of the noisy mob of dogs and street-boys who were laying siege to the door.

With the utmost caution he crawled along the roof-tree, trembling lest he should be discovered by some lynx-eyed villain in the throng of his pursuers. Happily, the broad brick chimney afforded him some shelter, of which he was quick to take advantage. Rolling himself up into the smallest possible compass, he sat for a long time crouching behind the chimney; while the police were rummaging under the beds and in the closets of the house, in the hope of finding him.

He had, of course, carefully closed the trap-door by which he had reached the comparative safety of his present position; and he could not help chuckling to himself at the thought of having outwitted the officers of the law.

The crowd outside, after having made night hideous by their whoops and yells, began, at the end of an hour, to grow weary; and the dogs being denied entrance to the house, concluded that they had no further business there, and slunk off to their respective kennels.

The people, too, scattered, and only a few patient loiterers hung about the street door, hoping for fresh developments. It seemed useless to Paul to wait until these provoking fellows should take themselves away. They were obviously prepared to make a night of it, and time was no object to them.

It was then that Paul, in his despair, resolved upon a daring stratagem. Mr. Broby's house was in the same block as that of the Misses Hansen, only it was at the other end of the block. By creeping along the roof-trees of the houses, which, happily, differed but slightly in height, he could reach the Broby house, where, no doubt, Miss Clara was now waiting for him, full of impatience.

He did not deliberate long before testing the practicability of this plan. The tanner Thoresen's house was reached without accident, although he barely escaped being detected by a small boy who was amusing himself throwing snow-balls at the chimney. It was a slow and wearisome mode of locomotion—pushing himself forward on his belly; but, as long as the streets were deserted, it was a pretty safe one.

He gave a start whenever he heard a dog bark; for the echoes of the ear-splitting concert they had given him were yet ringing in his brain.

It was no joke being a bear, he thought, and if he had suspected that it was such a serious business, he would not so rashly have undertaken it. But now there was no way of getting out of it; for he had nothing on but his underclothes under the bear-skin.

At last he reached the Broby house, and drew a sigh of relief at the thought that he was now at the end of his journey.

He looked about him for a trap-door by which he could descend into the interior, but could find none. There was an inch of snow on the roof, glazed with frost: and if there was a trap-door, it was securely hidden.

To jump or slide down was out of the question, for he would, in that case, risk breaking his neck. If he cried for help, the groom, who was always ready with his gun, might take a fancy to shoot at him; and that would be still more unpleasant. It was a most embarrassing situation.

Paul's eyes fell upon a chimney; and the thought flashed through his head that there was the solution of the difficulty. He observed that no smoke was coming out of it, so that he would run no risk of being converted into smoked ham during the descent.

He looked down through the long, black tunnel. It was a great, spacious, old-fashioned chimney, and abundantly wide enough for his purpose.

A pleasant sound of laughter and merry voices came to him from the kitchen below. It was evident the girls were having a frolic. So, without further ado, Paul Jespersen stuffed his great hairy bulk into the chimney and proceeded to let himself down.

There were notches and iron rings in the brick wall, evidently put there for the convenience of the chimney-sweeps; and he found his task easier than he had anticipated. The soot, to be sure, blinded his eyes, but where there was nothing to be seen, that was no serious disadvantage.

In fact, everything was going as smoothly as possible, when suddenly he heard a girl's voice cry out:

"Gracious goodness! what is that in the chimney? "

"Probably the chimney-sweep, " a man's voice answered.

"Chimney-sweep at this time of night! "

Paul, bracing himself against the walls, looked down and saw a cluster of anxious faces all gazing up toward him. A candle which one of the girls held in her hand showed him that the distance down to the hearth was but short; so, to make an end of their uncertainty, he dropped himself down—quietly, as he thought, but by the force of his fall blowing the ashes about in all directions.

A chorus of terrified screams greeted him. One girl fainted, one leaped up on a table, and the rest made for the door.

And there sat poor Paul, in the ashes on the hearth, utterly bewildered by the consternation he had occasioned. He picked himself up by and by, rubbed the soot out of his eyes with the backs of his paws, and crawled out upon the floor.

He had just managed to raise himself upon his hind-legs, when an awful apparition became visible in the door, holding a candle. It was now Paul's turn to be frightened. The person who stood before him bore a close resemblance to the devil.

"What is all this racket about? " he cried, in a tone of authority.

Paul felt instantly relieved, for the voice was that of his revered chief, Mr. Broby, who, he now recollected, was to figure at the masquerade as Mephistopheles. Behind him peeped forth the faces of his two daughters, one as Morning and the other as Spring.

"May I ask what is the cause of this unseemly noise? " repeated Mr. Broby, advancing to the middle of the room. The light of his candle now fell upon the huge bear whom, after a slight start, he recognized as a masker.

"Excuse me, Mr. Broby, " said Paul, "but Miss Clara did me the honor— —"

"Oh yes, papa, " Miss Clara interrupted him, stepping forth in all her glory of tulle and flowers; "it is Paul Jespersen, who was going to be my Beast. "

"And it is you who have frightened my servants half out of their wits, Jespersen? " said Mr. Broby, laughing.

"He tumbled down through the chimney, sir, " declared the cook, who had half-recovered from her fright.

"Well, " said Mr. Broby, with another laugh, "I admit that was a trifle unconventional. Next time you call, Jespersen, you must come through the door. "

He thought Jespersen had chosen to play a practical joke on the servants, and, though he did not exactly like it, he was in no mood for scolding. After having been carefully brushed and rolled in the snow, Paul offered his escort to Miss Clara; and she had not the heart to tell him that she was not at all Beauty, but Spring. And Paul was not enough of an expert to know the difference.

LADY CLARE
THE STORY OF A HORSE

The king was dead, and among the many things he left behind him which his successor had no use for were a lot of fancy horses. There were long-barrelled English hunters, all legs and neck; there were Kentucky racers, graceful, swift, and strong; and two Arabian steeds, which had been presented to his late majesty by the Sultan of Turkey. To see the beautiful beasts prancing and plunging, as they were being led through the streets by grooms in the royal livery, was enough to make the blood dance in the veins of any lover of horse-flesh. And to think that they were being led ignominiously to the auction mart to be sold under the hammer—knocked down to the highest bidder! It was a sin and a shame surely! And they seemed to feel it themselves; and that was the reason they acted so obstreperously, sometimes lifting the grooms off their feet as they reared and snorted and struck sparks with their steel-shod hoofs from the stone pavement.

Among the crowd of schoolboys who followed the equine procession, shrieking and yelling with glee and exciting the horses by their wanton screams, was a handsome lad of fourteen, named Erik Carstens. He had fixed his eyes admiringly on a coal-black, four-year-old mare, a mere colt, which brought up the rear of the procession. How exquisitely she was fashioned! How she danced over the ground with a light mazurka step, as if she were shod with gutta-percha and not with iron! And then she had a head so daintily shaped, small and spirited, that it was a joy to look at her. Erik, who, in spite of his youth, was not a bad judge of a horse, felt his heart beat like a trip-hammer, and a mighty yearning took possession of him to become the owner of that mare.

Though he knew it was time for dinner he could not tear himself away, but followed the procession up one street and down another, until it stopped at the horse market. There a lot of jockeys and coarse-looking dealers were on hand; and an opportunity was afforded them to try the horses before the auction began. They forced open the mouths of the beautiful animals, examined their teeth, prodded them with whips to see if they were gentle, and poked them with their fingers or canes. But when a loutish fellow, in a brown corduroy suit, indulged in that kind of behavior toward the black mare she gave a resentful whinny and without further ado grabbed him with her teeth by the coat collar, lifted him up and shook him as if he had been a bag of straw. Then she dropped him in the mud, and raised her dainty head with an air as if to say that she held him to be beneath contempt. The fellow, however, was not inclined to put up with that kind of treatment. With a volley of oaths he sprang up and would have struck the mare in the mouth with his clinched fist, if Erik had not darted forward and warded off the blow.

"How dare you strike that beautiful creature? " he cried, indignantly.

"Hold your jaw, you gosling, or I'll hit you instead, " retorted the man.

But by that time one of the royal grooms had made his appearance and the brute did not dare carry out his threat. While the groom strove to quiet the mare, a great tumult arose in some other part of the market-place. There was a whinnying, plunging, rearing, and screaming, as if the whole field had gone mad. The black mare joined in the concert, and stood with her ears pricked up and her head raised in an attitude of panicky expectation. Quite fearlessly Erik walked up to her, patted her on the neck and spoke soothingly to her.

"Look out, " yelled the groom, "or she'll trample you to jelly! "

But instead of that, the mare rubbed her soft nose against the boy's cheek, with a low, friendly neighing, as if she wished to thank him for his gallant conduct. And at that moment Erik's heart went out to that dumb creature with an affection which he had never felt toward any living thing before. He determined, whatever might happen, to bid on her and to buy her, whatever she might prove to be worth. He knew he had a few thousand dollars in the bank—his inheritance from his mother, who had died when he was a baby—and he might, perhaps, be able to persuade his father to sanction the purchase. At any rate, he would have some time to invent ways and means; for his father, Captain Carstens, was now away on the great annual drill, and would not return for some weeks.

As a mere matter of form, he resolved to try the mare before bidding on her; and slipping a coin into the groom's hand he asked for a saddle. It turned out, however, that all the saddles were in use, and Erik had no choice but to mount bareback.

"Ride her on the snaffle. She won't stand the curb, " shouted the groom, as the mare, after plunging to the right and to the left, darted through the gate to the track, and, after kicking up a vast deal of tan-bark, sped like a bullet down the race-course.

"Good gracious, how recklessly that boy rides! " one jockey observed to another; "but he has got a good grip with his knees all the same. "

"Yes, he sits like a daisy, " the second replied, critically; "but mind my word, Lady Clare will throw him yet. She never could stand anybody but the princess on her back: and that was the reason her Royal Highness was so fond of her. Mother of Moses, won't there be a grand rumpus when she comes back again and finds Lady Clare gone! I should not like to be in the shoes of the man who has ordered Lady Clare under the hammer. "

"But look at the lad! I told you Lady Clare wouldn't stand no manner of nonsense from boys. "

"She is kicking like a Trojan! She'll make hash of him if he loses his seat. "

"Yes, but he sticks like a burr. That's a jewel of a lad, I tell ye. He ought to have been a jockey. "

Up the track came Lady Clare, black as the ace of spades, acting like the Old Harry. Something had displeased her, obviously, and she held Erik responsible for it. Possibly she had just waked up to the fact that she, who had been the pet of a princess, was now being ridden by an ordinary commoner. At all events, she had made up her mind to get rid of the commoner without further ceremony. Putting her fine ears back and dilating her nostrils, she suddenly gave a snort and a whisk with her tail, and up went her heels toward the eternal stars—that is, if there had been any stars visible just then. Everybody's heart stuck in his throat; for fleet-footed racers were speeding round and round, and the fellow who got thrown in the midst of all these trampling hoofs would have small chance of looking upon the sun again. People instinctively tossed their heads up to see how high he would go before coming down again; but, for a wonder, they saw nothing, except a cloud of dust mixed with tan-bark, and when that had cleared away they discovered the black mare and her rider, apparently on the best of terms, dashing up the track at a breakneck pace.

Erik was dripping with perspiration when he dismounted, and Lady Clare's glossy coat was flecked with foam. She was not aware, apparently, that if she had any reputation to ruin she had damaged it most effectually. Her behavior on the track and her treatment of the horse-dealer were by this time common property, and every dealer and fancier made a mental note that Lady Clare was the number in the catalogue which he would not bid on. All her beauty and her distinguished ancestry counted for nothing, as long as she had so uncertain a temper. Her sire, Potiphar, it appeared, had also been subject to the same infirmities of temper, and there was a strain of savagery in her blood which might crop out when you least expected it.

Accordingly, when a dozen fine horses had been knocked down at good prices, and Lady Clare's turn came, no one came forward to inspect her, and no one could be found to make a bid.

"Well, well, gentlemen, " cried the auctioneer, "here we have a beautiful thoroughbred mare, the favorite mount of Her Royal Highness the Princess, and not a bid do I hear. She's a beauty, gentlemen, sired by the famous Potiphar who won the Epsom Handicap and no end of minor stakes. Take a look at her, gentlemen! Did you ever see a horse before that was raven black from nose to tail? I reckon you never did. But such a horse is Lady Clare. The man who can find a single white hair on her can have her for a gift. Come forward, gentlemen, come forward. Who will start her—say at five hundred? "

A derisive laugh ran through the crowd, and a voice was heard to cry, "Fifty. "

"Fifty! " repeated the auctioneer, in a deeply grieved and injured tone; "fifty did you say, sir? Fifty? Did I hear rightly? I hope, for the sake of the honor of this fair city, that my ears deceived me. "

Here came a long and impressive pause, during which the auctioneer, suddenly abandoning his dramatic manner, chatted familiarly with a gentleman who stood near him. The only one in the crowd whom he had impressed with the fact that the honor of the city was at stake in this sale was Erik Carstens. He had happily discovered a young and rich lieutenant of his father's company, and was trying to persuade him to bid in the mare for him.

"But, my dear boy, " Lieutenant Thicker exclaimed, "what do you suppose the captain will say to me if I aid and abet his son in defying the paternal authority? "

"Oh, you needn't bother about that, " Erik rejoined eagerly. "If father was at home, I believe he would allow me to buy this mare.

But I am a minor yet, and the auctioneer would not accept my bid.

Therefore I thought you might be kind enough to bid for me. "

The lieutenant made no answer, but looked at the earnest face of the boy with unmistakable sympathy. The auctioneer assumed again an insulted, affronted, pathetically entreating or scornfully repelling tone, according as it suited his purpose; and the price of Lady Clare crawled slowly and reluctantly up from fifty to seventy dollars. There it stopped, and neither the auctioneer's tears nor his prayers could apparently coax it higher.

"Seventy dollars! " he cried, as if he were really too shocked to speak at all; "seven-ty dollars! Make it eighty! Oh, it is a sin and a shame, gentlemen, and the fair fame of this beautiful city is eternally ruined. It will become a wagging of the head and a byword among the nations. Sev-en-ty dollars! " — then hotly and indignantly — "seventy dollars! —fifth and last time, seventy dollars! " — here he raised his hammer threateningly — "seventy dollars! "

"One hundred! " cried a high boyish voice, and in an instant every neck was craned and every eye was turned toward the corner where Erik Carstens was standing, half hidden behind the broad figure of Lieutenant Thicker.

"Did I hear a hundred? " repeated the auctioneer, wonderingly. "May I ask who was the gentleman who said a hundred? "

An embarrassing silence followed. Erik knew that if he acknowledged the bid he would suffer the shame of having it refused. But his excitement and his solicitude for the fair fame of his native city had carried him away so completely that the words had escaped from his lips before he was fully aware of their import.

"May I ask, " repeated the wielder of the hammer, slowly and emphatically, "may I ask the gentleman who offered one hundred dollars for Lady Clare to come forward and give his name? "

He now looked straight at Erik, who blushed to the edge of his hair, but did not stir from the spot. From sheer embarrassment he clutched the lieutenant's arm, and almost pinched it.

"Oh, I beg your pardon, " the officer exclaimed, addressing the auctioneer, as if he had suddenly been aroused from a fit of abstraction; "I made the bid of one hundred dollars, or—or—at any rate, I make it now. "

The same performance, intended to force up the price, was repeated once more, but with no avail, and at the end of two minutes Lady Clare was knocked down to Lieutenant Thicker.

"Now I have gone and done it like the blooming idiot that I am, " observed the lieutenant, when Lady Clare was led into his stable by a liveried groom. "What an overhauling the captain will give me when he gets home. "

"You need have no fear, " Erik replied. "I'll sound father as soon as he gets home; and if he makes any trouble I'll pay you that one hundred dollars, with interest, the day I come of age. "

Well, the captain came home, and having long had the intention to present his son with a saddle-horse, he allowed himself to be cajoled into approving of the bargain. The mare was an exquisite creature, if ever there was one, and he could well understand how Erik had been carried away; Lieutenant Thicker, instead of being hauled over the coals, as he had expected, received thanks for his kind and generous conduct toward the son of his superior officer. As for Erik himself, he had never had any idea that a boy's life could be so glorious as his was now. Mounted on that splendid, coal-black mare, he rode through the city and far out into the country at his father's side; and never did it seem to him that he had loved his father so well as he did during these afternoon rides. The captain was far from suspecting that in that episode of the purchase of Lady Clare his own relation to his son had been at stake. Not that Erik would not have obeyed his father, even if he had turned out his rough side and taken the lieutenant to task for his kindness; but their relation would in that case have lacked the warm intimacy (which in nowise excludes obedience and respect) and that last touch of devoted admiration which now bound them together.

That fine touch of sympathy in the captain's disposition which had enabled him to smile indulgently at his son's enthusiasm for the horse made the son doubly anxious not to abuse such kindness, and to do everything in his power to deserve the confidence which made his life so rich and happy. Though, as I have said, Captain Carstens lacked the acuteness to discover how much he owed to Lady Clare, he acknowledged himself in quite a different way her debtor. He had never really been aware what a splendid specimen of a boy his son was until he saw him on the back of that spirited mare, which cut up with him like the Old Harry, and yet never succeeded in flurrying, far less in unseating him. The captain felt a glow of affection warming his breast at the sight of this, and his pride in Erik's horsemanship proved a consolation to him when the boy's less distinguished performances at school caused him fret and worry.

"A boy so full of pluck must amount to something, even if he does not take kindly to Latin, " he reflected many a time. "I am afraid I have made a mistake in having him prepared for college. In the army now, and particularly in the cavalry, he would make a reputation in twenty minutes. "

And a cavalryman Erik might, perhaps, have become if his father had not been transferred to another post, and compelled to take up his residence in the country. It was nominally a promotion, but Captain Carstens was ill pleased with it, and even had some thought of resigning rather than give up his delightful city life, and move far northward into the region of cod and herring. However, he was too young a man to retire on a pension, as yet, and so he gradually reconciled himself to the thought, and sailed northward in the month of April with his son and his entire household. It had long been a question whether Lady Clare should make the journey with them; for Captain Carstens maintained that so high-bred an animal would be very sensitive to climatic changes and might even die on the way. Again, he argued that it was an absurdity to bring so fine a horse into a rough country, where the roads are poor and where nature, in mercy, provides all beasts with rough, shaggy coats to protect them from the cold. How would Lady Clare, with her glossy satin coat, her slender legs that pirouetted so daintily over the ground, and her exquisite head, which she carried so proudly—how would she look and what kind of figure would she cut among the shaggy, stunted, sedate-looking nags of the Sognefiord district? But the captain, though what he said was irrefutable, had to suspend all argument when he saw how utterly wretched Erik became at the mere thought of losing Lady Clare. So he took his chances; and, after having ordered blankets of three different thicknesses for three different kinds of weather, shipped the mare with the rest of his family for his new northern home.

As the weather proved unusually mild during the northward voyage Lady Clare arrived in Sogn without accident or adventure. And never in all her life had she looked more beautiful than she did when she came off the steamer, and half the population of the valley turned out to see her. It is no use denying that she was as vain as any other professional beauty, and the way she danced and pirouetted on the gangplank, when Erik led her on to the pier, filled the rustics with amazement. They had come to look at the new captain and his family; but when Lady Clare appeared she eclipsed the rest of the company so completely that no one had eyes for anybody but her. As the sun was shining and the wind was mild, Erik had taken off her striped overcoat (which covered her from nose to tail), for he felt in every fibre of his body the sensation she was making, and blushed with pleasure as if the admiring exclamations had been intended for himself.

"Look at that horse, " cried young and old, with eyes as big as saucers, pointing with their fingers at Lady Clare.

"Handsome carcass that mare has, " remarked a stoutish man, who knew what he was talking about; "and head and legs to match. "

"She beats your Valders-Roan all hollow, John Garvestad, " said a young tease who stood next to him in the crowd.

"My Valders-Roan has never seen his match yet, and never will, according to my reckoning, " answered John Garvestad.

"Ho! ho! " shouted the young fellow, with a mocking laugh; "that black mare is a hand taller at the very least, and I bet you she's a high-flyer. She has got the prettiest legs I ever clapped eyes on. "

"They'd snap like clay pipes in the mountains, " replied Garvestad, contemptuously.

Erik, as he blushingly ascended the slope to his new home, leading Lady Clare by a halter, had no suspicion of the sentiments which she had aroused in John Garvestad's breast. He was only blissfully conscious of the admiration she had excited; and he promised himself a good deal of fun in future in showing off his horsemanship. He took Lady Clare to the stable, where a new box-stall had been made for her, examined the premises carefully and nailed a board over a crevice in the wall where he suspected a draught. He instructed Anders, the groom, with emphatic and anxious repetitions regarding her care, showed him how to make Lady Clare's bed, how to comb her mane, how to brush her (for she refused to endure currying), how to blanket her, and how to read the thermometer which he nailed to one of the posts of the stall. The latter proved to be a more difficult task than he had anticipated; and the worst of it was that he was not sure that Anders knew any more on the subject of his instruction at the end of the lesson than he had at the beginning. To make sure that he had understood him he asked him to enter the stall and begin the process of grooming. But no sooner had the unhappy fellow put his nose inside the door than Lady Clare laid back her ears in a very ugly fashion, and with a vicious whisk of her tail waltzed around and planted two hoof-marks in the door, just where the groom's nose had that very instant vanished. A second and a third trial had similar results; and as the box-stall was new and of hard wood, Erik had no wish to see it further damaged.

"I won't have nothin' to do with that hoss, that's as certain as my name is Anders, " the groom declared; and Erik, knowing that persuasion would be useless, had henceforth to be his own groom. The fact was he could not help sympathizing with that fastidiousness of Lady Clare which made her object to be handled by coarse fingers and roughly curried, combed, and washed like a common plebeian nag. One does not commence life associating with a princess for nothing. Lady Clare, feeling in every nerve her high descent and breeding, had perhaps a sense of having come down in the world, and, like many another irrational creature of her sex, she kicked madly against fate and exhibited the unloveliest side of her character. But with all her skittishness and caprice she was steadfast in one thing, and that was her love for Erik. As the days went by in country monotony, he began to feel it as a privilege rather than a burden to have the exclusive care of her. The low, friendly neighing with which she always greeted him, as soon as he opened the stable-door, was as intelligible and dear to him as the warm welcome of a friend. And when with dainty alertness she lifted her small, beautiful head, over which the fine net-work of veins meandered, above the top of the stall, and rubbed her nose caressingly against his cheek, before beginning to snuff at his various pockets for the accustomed lump of sugar, he felt a glow of affection spread from his heart and pervade his whole being. Yes, he loved this beautiful animal with a devotion which, a year ago, he would scarcely have thought it possible to bestow upon a horse. No one could have persuaded him that Lady Clare had not a soul which (whether it was immortal or not) was, at all events, as distinct and clearly defined as that of any person with whom he was acquainted. She was to him a personality—a dear, charming friend, with certain defects of character (as who has not?) which were, however, more than compensated for by her devotion to him. She was fastidious, quick-tempered, utterly unreasonable where her feelings were involved; full of aristocratic prejudice, which only her sex could excuse; and whimsical, proud, and capricious. It was absurd, of course, to contend that these qualities were in themselves admirable; but, on the other hand, few of us would not consent to overlook them in a friend who loved us as well as Lady Clare loved Erik.

The fame of Lady Clare spread through the parish like fire in withered grass. People came from afar to look at her, and departed full of wonder at her beauty. When the captain and his son rode together to church on Sunday morning, men, women, and children stood in rows at the roadside staring at the wonderful mare as if she had been a dromedary or a rhinoceros. And when she was tied in the clergyman's stable a large number of the men ignored the admonition of the church bells and missed the sermon, being unable to tear themselves away from Lady Clare's charms. But woe to him who attempted to take liberties with her; there were two or three horsy young men who had narrow escapes from bearing the imprint of her iron shoes for the rest of their days.

That taught the others a lesson, and now Lady Clare suffered from no annoying familiarities, but was admired at a respectful distance, until the pastor, vexed at her rivalry with his sermon, issued orders to have the stable-door locked during service.

There was one person besides the pastor who was ill pleased at the reputation Lady Clare was making. That was John Garvestad, the owner of Valders-Roan. John was the richest man in the parish, and always made a point of keeping fine horses. Valders-Roan, a heavily built, powerful horse, with a tremendous neck and chest and long tassels on his fetlocks, but rather squat in the legs, had hitherto held undisputed rank as the finest horse in all Sogn. By the side of Lady Clare he looked as a stout, good-looking peasant lad with coltish manners might have looked by the side of the daughter of a hundred earls.

But John Garvestad, who was naturally prejudiced in favor of his own horse, could scarcely be blamed for failing to recognize her superiority. He knew that formerly, on Sundays, the men were wont to gather with admiring comment about Valders-Roan; while now they stood craning their necks, peering through the windows of the parson's stable, in order to catch a glimpse of Lady Clare, and all the time Valders-Roan was standing tied to the fence, in full view of all, utterly neglected. This spectacle filled him with such ire that he hardly could control himself. His first impulse was to pick a quarrel with Erik; but a second and far brighter idea presently struck him. He would buy Lady Clare. Accordingly, when the captain and his son had mounted their horses and were about to start on their homeward way, Garvestad, putting Valders-Roan to his trumps, dug his heels into his sides and rode up with a great flourish in front of the churchyard gate.

"How much will you take for that mare of yours, captain? " he asked, as he checked his charger with unnecessary vigor close to Lady Clare.

"She is not mine to sell, " the captain replied. "Lady Clare belongs to my son. "

"Well, what will you take for her, then? " Garvestad repeated, swaggeringly, turning to Erik.

"Not all the gold in the world could buy her, " retorted Erik, warmly.

Valders-Roan, unable to resist the charms of Lady Clare, had in the meanwhile been making some cautious overtures toward an acquaintance. He arched his mighty neck, rose on his hind legs, while his tremendous forehoofs were beating the air, and cut up generally—all for Lady Clare's benefit.

She, however, having regarded his performances for awhile with a mild and somewhat condescending interest, grew a little tired of them and looked out over the fiord, as a belle might do, with a suppressed yawn, when her cavalier fails to entertain her. Valders-Roan, perceiving the slight, now concluded to make more decided advances. So he put forward his nose until it nearly touched Lady Clare's, as if he meant to kiss her. But that was more than her ladyship was prepared to put up with. Quick as a flash she flung herself back on her haunches, down went her ears, and hers was the angriest horse's head that ever had been seen in that parish. With an indignant snort she wheeled around, kicking up a cloud of dust by the suddenness of the manoeuvre. A less skilled rider than Erik would inevitably have been thrown by two such unforeseen jerks; and the fact was he had all he could do to keep his seat.

"Oho! " shouted Garvestad, "your mare shies; she'll break your neck some day, as likely as not. You had better sell her before she gets you into trouble. "

"But I shouldn't like to have your broken neck on my conscience, " Erik replied; "if necks are to be broken by Lady Clare I should prefer to have it be my own. "

The peasant was not clever enough to make out whether this was jest or earnest. With a puzzled frown he stared at the youth and finally broke out:

"Then you won't sell her at no price? Anyway, the day you change your mind don't forget to notify John Garvestad. If it's spondulix you are after, then here's where there's plenty of 'em. "

He slapped his left breast-pocket with a great swagger, looking around to observe the impression he was making on his audience; then, jerking the bridle violently, so as to make his horse rear, he rode off like Alexander on Bucephalus, and swung down upon the highway.

It was but a few weeks after this occurrence that Captain Carstens and his son were invited to honor John Garvestad by their presence at his wedding. They were in doubt, at first, as to whether they ought to accept the invitation; for some unpleasant rumors had reached them, showing that Garvestad entertained unfriendly feelings toward them. He was an intensely vain man; and the thought that Erik Carstens had a finer horse than Valders-Roan left him no peace. He had been heard to say repeatedly that, if that high-nosed youth persisted in his refusal to sell the mare, he would discover his mistake when, perhaps, it would be too late to have it remedied. Whatever that meant, it sufficed to make both Erik and his father uneasy. But, on the other hand, it would be the worst policy possible, under such circumstances, to refuse the invitation. For that would be interpreted either as fear or as aristocratic exclusiveness; and the captain, while he was new in the district, was as anxious to avoid the appearance of the one as of the other. Accordingly he accepted the invitation and on the appointed day rode with his son into the wide yard of John Garvestad's farm, stopping at the pump, where they watered their horses. It was early in the afternoon, and both the house and the barn were thronged with wedding-guests. From the sitting-room the strains of two fiddles were heard, mingled with the scraping and stamping of heavy feet.

Another musical performance was in progress in the barn; and all over the yard elderly men and youths were standing in smaller and larger groups, smoking their pipes and tasting the beer-jugs, which were passed from hand to hand. But the moment Lady Clare was seen all interest in minor concerns ceased, and with one accord the crowd moved toward her, completely encircling her, and viewing her with admiring glances that appreciated all her perfections.

"Did you ever see cleaner-shaped legs on a horse? " someone was heard to say, and instantly his neighbor in the crowd joined the chorus of praise, and added: "What a snap and spring there is in every bend of her knee and turn of her neck and flash of her eye! "

It was while this chorus of admiration was being sung in all keys and tones of the whole gamut, that the bridegroom came out of the house, a little bit tipsy, perhaps, from the many toasts he had been obliged to drink, and bristling with pugnacity to the ends of his fingers and the tips of his hair. Every word of praise that he heard sounded in his ears like a jeer and an insult to himself. With ruthless thrusts he elbowed his way through the throng of guests and soon stood in front of the two horses, from which the captain and Erik had not yet had a chance to dismount. He returned their greeting with scant courtesy and plunged instantly into the matter which he had on his mind.

"I reckon you have thought better of my offer by this time, " he said, with a surly swagger, to Erik. "What do you hold your mare at to-day? "

"I thought we had settled that matter once for all, " the boy replied, quietly. "I have no more intention of selling Lady Clare now than I ever had. "

"Then will ye trade her off for Valders-Roan? " ejaculated Garvestad, eagerly.

"No, I won't trade her for Valders-Roan or any other horse in creation. "

"Don't be cantankerous, now, young fellow, or you might repent of it. "

"I am not cantankerous. But I beg of you kindly to drop this matter. I came here, at your invitation, as a guest at your wedding, not for the purpose of trading horses. "

It was an incautious speech, and was interpreted by everyone present as a rebuke to the bridegroom for his violation of the rules of hospitality. The captain, anxious to avoid a row, therefore broke in, in a voice of friendly remonstrance: "My dear Mr. Garvestad, do let us drop this matter. If you will permit us, we should like to dismount and drink a toast to your health, wishing you a long life and much happiness. "

"Ah, yes, I understand your smooth palaver, " the bridegroom growled between his teeth. "I have stood your insolence long enough, and, by jingo, I won't stand it much longer. What will ye take for your mare, I say, or how much do you want to boot, if you trade her for Valders-Roan? "

He shouted the last words with furious emphasis, holding his clinched fist up toward Erik, and glaring at him savagely.

But now Lady Clare, who became frightened perhaps by the loud talk and violent gestures, began to rear and plunge, and by an unforeseen motion knocked against the bridegroom, so that he fell backward into the horse-trough under the pump, which was full of water. The wedding-guests had hardly time to realize what was happening when a great splash sent the water flying into their faces, and the burly form of John Garvestad was seen sprawling helplessly in the horse-trough. But then—then they realized it with a vengeance. And a laugh went up—a veritable storm of laughter—which swept through the entire crowd and re-echoed with a ghostly hilarity from the mountains. John Garvestad in the meanwhile had managed to pick himself out of the horse-trough, and while he stood snorting, spitting, and dripping, Captain Carstens and his son politely lifted their hats to him and rode away. But as they trotted out of the gate they saw their host stretch a big clinched fist toward them, and heard him scream with hoarse fury: "I'll make ye smart for that some day, so help me God! "

Lady Clare was not sent to the mountains in the summer, as are nearly all horses in the Norwegian country districts. She was left untethered in an enclosed home pasture about half a mile from the mansion. Here she grazed, rolled, kicked up her heels, and gambolled to her heart's content. During the long, bright summer nights, when the sun scarcely dips beneath the horizon and reappears in an hour, clothed in the breezy garments of morning, she was permitted to frolic, race, and play all sorts of improvised games with a shaggy, little, plebeian three-year-old colt whom she had condescended to honor with her acquaintance. This colt must have had some fine feeling under his rough coat, for he never presumed in the least upon the acquaintance, being perhaps aware of the honor it conferred upon him. He allowed himself to be abused, ignored, or petted, as it might suit the pleasure of her royal highness, with a patient, even-tempered good-nature which was admirable. When Lady Clare (perhaps for fear of making him conceited) took no notice of him, he showed neither resentment nor surprise, but walked off with a sheepish shake of his head. Thus he slowly learned the lesson to make no exhibition of feeling at the sight of his superior; not to run up and greet her with a disrespectfully joyous whinny; but calmly wait for her to recognize him before appearing to be aware of her presence. It took Lady Clare several months to accustom Shag (for that was the colt's name) to her ways. She taught him unconsciously the rudiments of good manners; but he proved himself docile, and when he once had been reduced to his proper place he proved a fairly acceptable companion.

During the first and second week after John Garvestad's wedding Erik had kept Lady Clare stabled, having a vague fear that the angry peasant might intend to do her harm. But she whinnied so pitifully through the long light nights that finally he allowed his compassion to get the better of his anxiety, and once more she was seen racing madly about the field with Shag, whom she always beat so ignominiously that she felt half sorry for him, and as a consolation allowed him gently to claw her mane with his teeth. This was a privilege which Shag could not fail to appreciate, though she never offered to return the favor by clawing him. At any rate, as soon as Lady Clare reappeared in the meadow Shag's cup of bliss seemed to be full.

A week passed in this way, nothing happened, and Erik's vigilance was relaxed. He went to bed on the evening of July 10th with an easy mind, without the remotest apprehension of danger. The sun set about ten o'clock, and Lady Clare and Shag greeted its last departing rays with a whinny, accompanied by a wanton kickup from the rear—for whatever Lady Clare did Shag felt in honor bound to do, and was conscious of no disgrace in his abject and ape-like imitation. They had spent an hour, perhaps, in such delightful performances, when all of a sudden they were startled by a deep bass whinny, which rumbled and shook like distant thunder. Then came the tramp, tramp, tramp of heavy hoof-beats, which made the ground tremble. Lady Clare lifted her beautiful head and looked with fearless curiosity in the direction whence the sound came. Shag, of course, did as nearly as he could exactly the same. What they saw was a big roan horse with an enormous arched neck, squat feet, and long-tasselled fetlocks.

Lady Clare had no difficulty in recognizing Valders-Roan. But how big and heavy and ominous he looked in the blood-red after-glow of the blood-red sunset. For the first time in her life Lady Clare felt a cold shiver of fear run through her. There was, happily, a fence between them, and she devoutly hoped that Valders-Roan was not a jumper. At that moment, however, two men appeared next to the huge horse, and Lady Clare heard the sound of breaking fence-rails. The deep hoarse whinny once more made the air shake, and it made poor Lady Clare shake too, for now she saw Valders-Roan come like a whirlwind over the field, and so powerful were his hoof-beats that a clod of earth which had stuck to one of his shoes shot like a bullet through the air.

He looked so gigantic, so brimming with restrained strength, and somehow Lady Clare, as she stood quaking at the sight of him, had never seemed to herself so dainty, frail, and delicate as she seemed in this moment. She felt herself so entirely at his mercy; she was no match for him surely. Shag, anxious as ever to take his cue from her, had stationed himself at her side, and shook his head and whisked his tail in a non-committal manner. Now Valders-Roan had cleared the fence where the men had broken it down; then on he came again, tramp, tramp, tramp, until he was within half a dozen paces from Lady Clare. There he stopped, for back went Lady Clare's pretty ears, while she threw herself upon her haunches in an attitude of defence. She was dimly aware that this was a foolish thing to do, but her inbred disdain and horror of everything rough made her act on instinct instead of reason. Valders-Roan, irritated by this uncalled-for action, now threw ceremony to the winds, and without further ado trotted up and rubbed his nose against hers. That was more than Lady Clare could stand. With an hysterical snort she flung herself about, and up flew her heels straight into the offending nose, inflicting considerable damage. Shag, being now quite clear that the programme was fight, whisked about in exactly the same manner, with as close an imitation of Lady Clare's snort as he could produce, and a second pair of steel-shod heels came within a hair of reducing the enemy's left nostril to the same condition as the right. But alas for the generous folly of youth! Shag had to pay dearly for that exhibition of devotion. Valders-Roan, enraged by this wanton insult, made a dash at Shag, and by the mere impetus of his huge bulk nearly knocked him senseless. The colt rolled over, flung all his four legs into the air, and as soon as he could recover his footing reeled sideways like a drunken man and made haste to retire to a safe distance.

Valders-Roan had now a clear field and could turn his undivided attention to Lady Clare. I am not sure that he had not made an example of Shag merely to frighten her. Bounding forward with his mighty chest expanded and the blood dripping from his nostrils, he struck out with a tremendous hind leg and would have returned Lady Clare's blow with interest if she had not leaped high into the air. She had just managed by her superior alertness to dodge that deadly hoof, and was perhaps not prepared for an instant renewal of the attack. But she had barely gotten her four feet in contact with the sod when two rows of terrific teeth plunged into her withers. The pain was frightful, and with a long, pitiful scream Lady Clare sank down upon the ground, and, writhing with agony, beat the air with her hoofs. Shag, who had by this time recovered his senses, heard the noise of the battle, and, plucking up his courage, trotted bravely forward against the victorious Valders-Roan. He was so frightened that his heart shot up into his throat. But there lay Lady Clare mangled and bleeding. He could not leave her in the lurch, so forward he came, trembling, just as Lady Clare was trying to scramble to her feet. Led away by his sympathy Shag bent his head down toward her and thereby prevented her from rising. And in the same instant a stunning blow hit him straight in the forehead, a shower of sparks danced before his eyes, and then Shag saw and heard no more. A convulsive quiver ran through his body, then he stretched out his neck on the bloody grass, heaved a sigh, and died.

Lady Clare, seeing Shag killed by the blow which had been intended for herself, felt her blood run cold. She was strongly inclined to run, for she could easily beat the heavy Valders-Roan at a race, and her fleet legs might yet save her. I cannot say whether it was a generous wrath at the killing of her humble champion or a mere blind fury which overcame this inclination. But she knew now neither pain nor fear. With a shrill scream she rushed at Valders-Roan, and for five minutes a whirling cloud of earth and grass and lumps of sod moved irregularly over the field, and tails, heads, and legs were seen flung and tossed madly about, while an occasional shriek of rage or of pain startled the night, and re-echoed with a weird resonance between the mountains.

It was about five o'clock in the morning of July 11th, that Erik awoke, with a vague sense that something terrible had happened. His groom was standing at his bedside with a terrified face, doubtful whether to arouse his young master or allow him to sleep.

"What has happened, Anders? " cried Erik, tumbling out of bed.

"Lady Clare, sir — —"

"Lady Clare! " shouted the boy. "What about her? Has she been stolen? "

"No, I reckon not, " drawled Anders.

"Then she's dead! Quick, tell me what you know or I shall go crazy!"

"No; I can't say for sure she's dead either, " the groom stammered, helplessly.

Erik, being too stunned with grief and pain, tumbled in a dazed fashion about the room, and scarcely knew how he managed to dress. He felt cold, shivery, and benumbed; and the daylight had a cruel glare in it which hurt his eyes. Accompanied by his groom, he hastened to the home pasture, and saw there the evidence of the fierce battle which had raged during the night. A long, black, serpentine track, where the sod had been torn up by furious hoof-beats, started from the dead carcass of the faithful Shag and moved with irregular breaks and curves up toward the gate that connected the pasture with the underbrush of birch and alder. Here the fence had been broken down, and the track of the fight suddenly ceased. A pool of blood had soaked into the ground, showing that one of the horses, and probably the victor, must have stood still for a while, allowing the vanquished to escape.

Erik had no need of being told that the horse which had attacked Lady Clare was Valders-Roan; and though he would scarcely have been able to prove it, he felt positive that John Garvestad had arranged and probably watched the fight. Having a wholesome dread of jail, he had not dared to steal Lady Clare; but he had chosen this contemptible method to satisfy his senseless jealousy. It was all so cunningly devised as to baffle legal inquiry. Valders-Roan had gotten astray, and being a heavy beast, had broken into a neighbor's field and fought with his filly, chasing her away into the mountains. That was the story he would tell, of course, and as there had been no witnesses present, there was no way of disproving it.

Abandoning, however, for the time being all thought of revenge, Erik determined to bend all his energies to the recovery of Lady Clare. He felt confident that she had run away from her assailant, and was now roaming about in the mountains. He therefore organized a search party of all the male servants on the estate, besides a couple of volunteers, making in all nine. On the evening of the first day's search they put up at a saeter or mountain chalet. Here they met a young man named Tollef Morud, who had once been a groom at John Garvestad's. This man had a bad reputation; and as the idea occurred to some of them that he might know something about Lady Clare's disappearance, they questioned him at great length, without, however, eliciting a single crumb of information.

For a week the search was continued, but had finally to be given up. Weary, footsore, and heavy hearted, Erik returned home. His grief at the loss of Lady Clare began to tell on his health; and his perpetual plans for getting even with John Garvestad amounted almost to a mania, and caused his father both trouble and anxiety. It was therefore determined to send him to the military academy in the capital.

Four or five years passed and Erik became a lieutenant. It was during the first year after his graduation from the military academy that he was invited to spend the Christmas holidays with a friend, whose parents lived on a fine estate about twenty miles from the city. Seated in their narrow sleighs, which were drawn by brisk horses, they drove merrily along, shouting to each other to make their voices heard above the jingling of the bells. About eight o'clock in the evening, when the moon was shining brightly and the snow sparkling, they turned in at a wayside tavern to order their supper. Here a great crowd of lumbermen had congregated, and all along the fences their overworked, half- broken-down horses stood, shaking their nose-bags. The air in the public room was so filled with the fumes of damp clothes and bad tobacco that Erik and his friend, while waiting for their meal, preferred to spend the time under the radiant sky. They were sauntering about, talking in a desultory fashion, when all of a sudden a wild, joyous whinny rang out upon the startled air.

It came from a rusty, black, decrepit-looking mare hitched to a lumber sleigh which they had just passed. Erik, growing very serious, paused abruptly.

A second whinny, lower than the first, but almost alluring and cajoling, was so directly addressed to Erik that he could not help stepping up to the mare and patting her on the nose.

"You once had a horse you cared a great deal for, didn't you? " his friend remarked, casually.

"Oh, don't speak about it, " answered Erik, in a voice that shook with emotion; "I loved Lady Clare as I never loved any creature in this world—except my father, of course, " he added, reflectively.

But what was the matter with the old lumber nag? At the sound of the name Lady Clare she pricked up her ears, and lifted her head with a pathetic attempt at alertness. With a low, insinuating neighing she rubbed her nose against the lieutenant's cheek. He had let his hand glide over her long, thin neck, when quite suddenly his fingers slid into a deep scar in the withers.

"My God! " he cried, while the tears started to his eyes, "am I awake, or am I dreaming? "

"What in the world is the matter? " inquired his comrade, anxiously.

"It is Lady Clare! By the heavens, it is Lady Clare! "

"That old ramshackle of a lumber nag whose every rib you can count through her skin is your beautiful thoroughbred? " ejaculated his friend, incredulously. "Come now, don't be a goose. "

"I'll tell you of it some other time, " said Erik, quietly; "but there's not a shadow of a doubt that this is Lady Clare. "

Yes, strange as it may seem, it was indeed Lady Clare. But oh, who would have recognized in this skeleton, covered with a rusty-black skin and tousled mane and forelock in which chaff and dirt were entangled—who would have recognized in this drooping and rickety creature the proud, the dainty, the exquisite Lady Clare? Her beautiful tail, which had once been her pride, was now a mere scanty wisp; and a sharp, gnarled ridge running along the entire length of her back showed every vertebra of her spine through the notched and scarred skin. Poor Lady Clare, she had seen hard usage. But now the days of her tribulations are at an end. It did not take Erik long to find the half-tipsy lumberman who was Lady Clare's owner; nor to agree with him on the price for which he was willing to part with her.

There is but little more to relate. By interviews and correspondence with the different parties through whose hands the mare had passed, Erik succeeded in tracing her to Tollef Morud, the ex-groom of John Garvestad. On being promised immunity from prosecution, he was induced to confess that he had been hired by his former master to arrange the nocturnal fight between Lady Clare and Valders-Roan, and had been paid ten dollars for stealing the mare when she had been sufficiently damaged. John Garvestad had himself watched the fight from behind the fence, and had laughed fit to split his sides, until Valders-Roan seemed on the point of being worsted. Then he had interfered to separate them, and Tollef had led Lady Clare away, bleeding from a dozen wounds, and had hidden her in a deserted lumberman's shed near the saeter where the searchers had overtaken him.

Having obtained these facts, Erik took pains to let John Garvestad know that the chain of evidence against him was complete, and if he had had his own way he would not have rested until his enemy had suffered the full penalty of the law. But John Garvestad, suspecting what was in the young man's mind, suddenly divested himself of his pride, and cringing dike a whipped dog, came and asked Erik's pardon, entreating him not to prosecute.

As for Lady Clare, she never recovered her lost beauty. A pretty fair-looking mare she became, to be sure, when good feeding and careful grooming had made her fat and glossy once more. A long and contented old age is, no doubt, in store for her. Having known evil days, she appreciates the blessings which the change in her fate has brought her. The captain declares she is the best-tempered and steadiest horse in his stable.

BONNYBOY

I.

"Oh, you never will amount to anything, Bonnyboy! " said Bonnyboy's father, when he had vainly tried to show him how to use a gouge; for Bonnyboy had just succeeded in gouging a piece out of his hand, and was standing helplessly, letting his blood drop on an engraving of Napoleon at Austerlitz, which had been sent to his father for framing. The trouble with Bonnyboy was that he was not only awkward—left-handed in everything he undertook, as his father put it—but he was so very good-natured that it was impossible to get angry with him. His large blue innocent eyes had a childlike wonder in them, when he had done anything particularly stupid, and he was so willing and anxious to learn, that his ill-success seemed a reason for pity rather than for wrath. Grim Norvold, Bonnyboy's father, was by trade a carpenter, and handy as he was at all kinds of tinkering, he found it particularly exasperating to have a son who was so left-handed. There was scarcely anything Grim could not do. He could take a watch apart and put it together again; he could mend a harness if necessary; he could make a wagon; nay, he could even doctor a horse when it got spavin or glanders. He was a sort of jack-of-all-trades, and a very useful man in a valley where mechanics were few and transportation difficult. He loved work for its own sake, and was ill at ease when he had not a tool in his hand. The exercise of his skill gave him a pleasure akin to that which the fish feels in swimming, the eagle in soaring, and the lark in singing. A finless fish, a wingless eagle, or a dumb lark could not have been more miserable than Grim was when a succession of holidays, like Easter or Christmas, compelled him to be idle.

When his son was born his chief delight was to think of the time when he should be old enough to handle a tool, and learn the secrets of his father's trade. Therefore, from the time the boy was old enough to sit or to crawl in the shavings without getting his mouth and eyes full of sawdust, he gave him a place under the turning bench, and talked or sang to him while he worked. And Bonnyboy, in the meanwhile amused himself by getting into all sorts of mischief. If it had not been for the belief that a good workman must grow up in the atmosphere of the shop, Grim would have lost patience with his son and sent him back to his mother, who had better facilities for taking care of him. But the fact was he was too fond of the boy to be able to dispense with him, and he would rather bear the loss resulting from his mischief than miss his prattle and his pretty dimpled face.

It was when the child was eighteen or nineteen months old that he acquired the name Bonnyboy. A woman of the neighborhood, who had called at the shop with some article of furniture which she wanted to have mended, discovered the infant in the act of investigating a pot of blue paint, with a part of which he had accidentally decorated his face.

"Good gracious! what is that ugly thing you have got under your turning bench? " she cried, staring at the child in amazement.

"No, he is not an ugly thing, " replied the father, with resentment; "he is a bonny boy, that's what he is. "

The woman, in order to mollify Grim, turned to the boy, and asked, with her sweetest manner, "What is your name, child? "

"Bonny boy, " murmured the child, with a vaguely offended air— "bonny boy. "

And from that day the name Bonnyboy clung to him.

II.

To teach Bonnyboy the trade of a carpenter was a task which would have exhausted the patience of all the saints in the calendar. If there was any possible way of doing a thing wrong, Bonnyboy would be sure to hit upon that way. When he was eleven years old he chopped off the third joint of the ring-finger on his right hand with a cutting tool while working the turning-lathe; and by the time he was fourteen it seemed a marvel to his father that he had any fingers left at all. But Bonnyboy persevered in spite of all difficulties, was always cheerful and of good courage, and when his father, in despair, exclaimed: "Well, you will never amount to anything, Bonnyboy, " he would look up with his slow, winning smile and say:

"Don't worry, father. Better luck next time. "

"But, my dear boy, how can I help worrying, when you don't learn anything by which you can make your living? "

"Oh, well, father, " said Bonnyboy, soothingly (for he was beginning to feel sorry on his father's account rather than on his own), "I wouldn't bother about that if I were you. I don't worry a bit. Something will turn up for me to do, sooner or later. "

"But you'll do it badly, Bonnyboy, and then you won't get a second chance. And then, who knows but you may starve to death. You'll chop off the fingers you have left; and when I am dead and can no longer look after you, I am very much afraid you'll manage to chop off your head too. "

"Well, " observed Bonnyboy, cheerfully, "in that case I shall not starve to death. "

Grim had to laugh in spite of himself at the paternal way in which his son comforted him, as if he were the party to be pitied. Bonnyboy's unfailing cheerfulness, which had its great charm, began to cause him uneasiness, because he feared it was but another form of stupidity. A cleverer boy would have been sorry for his mistakes and anxious about his own future. But Bonnyboy looked into the future with the serene confidence of a child, and nothing under the sun ever troubled him, except his father's tendency to worry. For he was very fond of his father, and praised him as a paragon of skill and excellence. He lavished an abject admiration on everything he did and said. His dexterity in the use of tools, and his varied accomplishments as a watch-maker and a horse-doctor, filled Bonnyboy with ungrudging amazement. He knew it was a hopeless thing for him to aspire to rival such genius, and he took the thing philosophically, and did not aspire.

It occurred to Grim one day, when Bonnyboy had made a most discouraging exhibition of his awkwardness, that it might be a good thing to ask the pastor's advice in regard to him. The pastor had had a long experience in educating children, and his own, though they were not all clever, promised to turn out well. Accordingly Grim called at the parsonage, was well received, and returned home charged to the muzzle with good advice. The pastor lent him a book full of stories, and recommended him to read them to his son, and afterward question him about every single fact which each story contained. This the pastor had found to be a good way to develop the intellect of a backward boy.

III.

When Bonnyboy had been confirmed, the question again rose what was to become of him. He was now a tall young fellow, red-cheeked, broad-shouldered, and strong, and rather nice-looking. A slow, good-natured smile spread over his face when anyone spoke to him, and he had a way of flinging his head back, when the tuft of yellow hair which usually hung down over his forehead obscured his sight. Most people liked him, even though they laughed at him behind his back; but to his face nobody laughed, because his strength inspired respect. Nor did he know what fear was when he was roused; but that was probably, as people thought, because he did not know much of anything. At any rate, on a certain occasion he showed that there was a limit to his good-nature, and when that limit was reached, he was not as harmless a fellow as he looked.

On the neighboring farm of Gimlehaug there was a wedding to which Grim and his son were invited. On the afternoon of the second wedding day—for peasant weddings in Norway are often celebrated for three days—a notorious bully named Ola Klemmerud took it into his head to have some sport with the big good-natured simpleton. So, by way of pleasantry, he pulled the tuft of hair which hung down upon Bonnyboy's forehead.

"Don't do that, " said Bonnyboy.

Ola Klemmerud chuckled, and the next time he passed Bonnyboy, pinched his ear.

"If you do that again I sha'n't like you, " cried Bonnyboy.

The innocence of that remark made the people laugh, and the bully, seeing that their sympathy was on his side, was encouraged to continue his teasing. Taking a few dancing steps across the floor, he managed to touch Bonnyboy's nose with the toe of his boot, which feat again was rewarded with a burst of laughter. The poor lad quietly blew his nose, wiped the perspiration off his brow with a red handkerchief, and said, "Don't make me mad, Ola, or I might hurt you. "

This speech struck the company as being immensely funny, and they laughed till the tears ran down their cheeks. At this moment Grim entered, and perceived at once that Ola Klemmerud was amusing the company at his son's expense. He grew hot about his ears, clinched his teeth, and stared challengingly at the bully. The latter began to feel uncomfortable, but he could not stop at this point without turning the laugh against himself, and that he had not the courage to do. So in order to avoid rousing the father's wrath, and yet preserving his own dignity, he went over to Bonnyboy, rumpled his hair with both his hands, and tweaked his nose. This appeared such innocent sport, according to his notion, that no rational creature could take offence at it. But Grim, whose sense of humor was probably defective, failed to see it in that light.

"Let the boy alone, " he thundered.

"Well, don't bite my head off, old man, " replied Ola. "I haven't hurt your fool of a boy. I have only been joking with him. "

"I don't think you are troubled with overmuch wit yourself, judging by the style of your jokes, " was Grim's cool retort.

The company, who plainly saw that Ola was trying to wriggle out of his difficulty, but were anxious not to lose an exciting scene, screamed with laughter again; but this time at the bully's expense. The blood mounted to his head, and his anger got the better of his natural cowardice. Instead of sneaking off, as he had intended, he wheeled about on his heel and stood for a moment irresolute, clinching his fist in his pocket.

"Why don't you take your lunkhead of a son home to his mother, if he isn't bright enough to understand fun! " he shouted.

"Now let me see if you are bright enough to understand the same kind of fun, " cried Grim. Whereupon he knocked off Ola's cap, rumpled his hair, and gave his nose such a pull that it was a wonder it did not come off.

The bully, taken by surprise, tumbled a step backward, but recovering himself, struck Grim in the face with his clinched fist. At this moment. Bonnyboy, who had scarcely taken in the situation; jumped up and screamed, "Sit down, Ola Klemmerud, sit down! "

The effect of this abrupt exclamation was so comical, that people nearly fell from their benches as they writhed and roared with laughter.

Bonnyboy, who had risen to go to his father's assistance, paused in astonishment in the middle of the floor. He could not comprehend, poor boy, why everything he said provoked such uncontrollable mirth. He surely had no intention of being funny.

So, taken aback a little, he repeated to himself, half wonderingly, with an abrupt pause after each word, "Sit—down—Ola—Klemmerud—sit—down! "

But Ola Klemmerud, instead of sitting down, hit Grim repeatedly about the face and head, and it was evident that the elder man, in spite of his strength, was not a match for him in alertness. This dawned presently upon Bonnyboy's slow comprehension, and his good-natured smile gave way to a flush of excitement. He took two long strides across the floor, pushed his father gently aside, and stood facing his antagonist. He repeated once more his invitation to sit down; to which the latter responded with a slap which made the sparks dance before Bonnyboy's eyes. Now Bonnyboy became really angry. Instead of returning the slap, he seized his enemy with a sudden and mighty grab by both his shoulders, lifted him up as if he were a bag of hay, and put him down on a chair with such force that it broke into splinters under him.

"Will you now sit down? " said Bonnyboy.

Nobody laughed this time, and the bully, not daring to rise, remained seated on the floor among the ruins of the chair. Thereupon, with imperturbable composure, Bonnyboy turned to his father, brushed off his coat with his hands and smoothed his disordered hair. "Now let us go home, father, " he said, and taking the old man's arm he walked out of the room. But hardly had he crossed the threshold before the astonished company broke into cheering.

"Good for you, Bonnyboy! " "Well done, Bonnyboy! " "You are a bully boy, Bonnyboy! " they cried after him.

But Bonnyboy strode calmly along, quite unconscious of his triumph, and only happy to have gotten his father out of the room safe and sound. For a good while they walked on in silence. Then, when the effect of the excitement had begun to wear away, Grim stopped in the path, gazed admiringly at his son, and said, "Well, Bonnyboy, you are a queer fellow. "

"Oh, yes, " answered Bonnyboy, blushing with embarrassment (for though he did not comprehend the remark, he felt the approving gaze); "but then, you know, I asked him to sit down, and he wouldn't. "

"Bless your innocent heart! " murmured his father, as he gazed at Bonnyboy's honest face with a mingling of affection and pity.

IV.

When Bonnyboy was twenty years old his father gave up, once for all, his attempt to make a carpenter of him. A number of saw-mills had been built during the last years along the river down in the valley, and the old rapids had been broken up into a succession of mill-dams, one above the other. At one of these saw-mills Bonnyboy sought work, and was engaged with many others as a mill hand. His business was to roll the logs on to the little trucks that ran on rails, and to push them up to the saws, where they were taken in charge by another set of men, who fastened and watched them while they were cut up into planks. Very little art was, indeed, required for this simple task; but strength was required, and of this Bonnyboy had enough and to spare. He worked with a will from early morn till dewy eve, and was happy in the thought that he had at last found something that he could do. It made the simple-hearted fellow proud to observe that he was actually gaining his father's regard; or, at all events, softening the disappointment which, in a vague way, he knew that his dulness must have caused him. If, occasionally, he was hurt by a rolling log, he never let any one know it; but even though his foot was a mass of agony every time he stepped on it, he would march along as stiffly as a soldier. It was as if he felt his father's eye upon him long before he saw him.

There was a curious kind of sympathy between them which expressed itself, on the father's part, in a need to be near his son. But he feared to avow any such weakness, knowing that Bonnyboy would interpret it as distrust of his ability to take care of himself, and a desire to help him if he got into trouble. Grim, therefore, invented all kinds of transparent pretexts for paying visits to the saw-mills. And when he saw Bonnyboy, conscious that his eye was resting upon him, swinging his axe so that the chips flew about his ears, and the perspiration rained from his brow, a dim anxiety often took possession of him, though he could give no reason for it. That big brawny fellow, with the frame of a man and the brain of a child, with his guileless face and his guileless heart, strangely moved his compassion. There was something almost beautiful about him, his father thought; but he could not have told what it was; nor would he probably have found any one else that shared his opinion. That frank and genial gaze of Bonnyboy's, which expressed goodness of heart but nothing else, seemed to Grim an "open sesame" to all hearts; and that unawakened something which goes so well with childhood, but not with adult age, filled him with tenderness and a vague anxiety. "My poor lad, " he would murmur to himself, as he caught sight of Bonnyboy's big perspiring face, with the yellow tuft of hair hanging down over his forehead, "clever you are not; but you have that which the cleverest of us often lack. "

V.

There were sixteen saw-mills in all, and the one at which Bonnyboy was employed was the last of the series. They were built on little terraces on both banks of the river, and every four of them were supplied with power from an artificial dam, in which the water was stored in time of drought, and from which it escaped in a mill-race when required for use. These four dams were built of big stones, earthwork, and lumber, faced with smooth planks, over which a small quantity of water usually drizzled into the shallow river-bed. Formerly, before the power was utilized, this slope had been covered with seething and swirling rapids—a favorite resort of the salmon, which leaped high in the spring, and were caught in the box-traps that hung on long beams over the water. Now the salmon had small chance of shedding their spawn in the cool, bright mountain pools, for they could not leap the dams, and if by chance one got into the mill- race, it had a hopeless struggle against a current that would have carried an elephant off his feet. Bonnyboy, who more than once had seen the beautiful silvery fish spring right on to the millwheel, and be flung upon the rocks, had wished that he had understood the language of the fishes, so that he might tell them how foolish such proceedings were. But merciful though he was, he had been much discouraged when, after having put them back into the river, they had promptly repeated the experiment.

There were about twenty-five or thirty men employed at the mill where Bonnyboy earned his bread in the sweat of his brow, and he was, on the whole, on good terms with all of them. They did, to be sure, make fun of him occasionally; but sometimes he failed to understand it, and at other times he made clumsy but good-humored attempts to repay their gibes in kind. They took good care, however, not to rouse his wrath, for the reputation he had acquired by his treatment of Ola Klemmerud made them afraid to risk a collision.

This was the situation when the great floods of 188- came, and introduced a spice of danger into Bonnyboy's monotonous life. The mill-races were now kept open night and day, and yet the water burst like a roaring cascade over the tops of dams, and the river-bed was filled to overflowing with a swiftly-hurrying tawny torrent, which filled the air with its rush and swash, and sent hissing showers of spray flying through the tree-tops. Bonnyboy and a gang of twenty men were working as they had never worked before in their lives, under the direction of an engineer, who had been summoned by the mill-owner to strengthen the dams; for if but one of them burst, the whole tremendous volume of water would be precipitated upon the valley, and the village by the lower falls and every farm within half a mile of the river-banks would be swept out of existence. Guards were stationed all the way up the river to intercept any stray lumber that might be afloat. For if a log jam were added to the terrific strain of the flood, there would surely be no salvation possible. Yet in spite of all precautions, big logs now and then came bumping against the dams, and shot with wild gyrations and somersaults down into the brown eddies below.

The engineer, who was standing on the top of a log pile, had shouted until he was hoarse, and gesticulated with his cane until his arms were lame, but yet there was a great deal to do before he could go to bed with an easy conscience. Bonnyboy and his comrades, who had had by far the harder part of the task, were ready to drop with fatigue. It was now eight o'clock in the evening, and they had worked since six in the morning, and had scarcely had time to swallow their scant rations. Some of them began to grumble, and the engineer had to coax and threaten them to induce them to persevere for another hour. The moon was just rising behind the mountain ridges, and the beautiful valley lay, with its green fields, sprouting forests, and red-painted farm-houses, at Bonnyboy's feet. It was terrible to think that perhaps destruction was to overtake those happy and peaceful homes, where men had lived and died for many hundred years. Bonnyboy could scarcely keep back the tears when this fear suddenly came over him. Was it not strange that, though they knew that danger was threatening, they made not the slightest effort to save themselves? In the village below men were still working in their forges, whose chimneys belched forth fiery smoke, and the sound of their hammer-blows could be heard above the roar of the river. Women were busy with their household tasks; some boys were playing in the streets, damming up the gutters and shrieking with joy when their dams broke. A few provident souls had driven their cattle to the neighboring hills; but neither themselves nor their children had they thought it necessary to remove. The fact was, nobody believed that the dams would break, as they had not imagination enough to foresee what would happen if the dams did break.

Bonnyboy was wet to the skin, and his knees were a trifle shaky from exhaustion. He had been cutting down an enormous mast-tree, which was needed for a prop to the dam, and had hauled it down with two horses, one of which was a half-broken gray colt, unused to pulling in a team. To restrain this frisky animal had required all Bonnyboy's strength, and he stood wiping his brow with the sleeve of his shirt. Just at that moment a terrified yell sounded from above: "Run for your lives! The upper dam is breaking! "

The engineer from the top of the log-pile cast a swift glance up the valley, and saw at once from the increasing volume of water that the report was true.

"Save yourselves, lads! " he screamed. "Run to the woods! "

And suiting his action to his words, he tumbled down from the log pile, and darted up the hill-side toward the forest. The other men, hearing the wild rush and roar above them, lost no time in following his example. Only Bonnyboy, slow of comprehension as always, did not obey. Suddenly there flared up a wild resolution in his face. He pulled out his knife, cut the traces, and leaped upon the colt's back. Lashing the beast, and shouting at the top of his voice, he dashed down the hill-side at a break-neck pace.

"The dam is breaking! " he roared. "Run for the woods! "

He glanced anxiously behind him to see if the flood was overtaking him. A great cloud of spray was rising against the sky, and he heard the yells of men and the frenzied neighing of horses through the thunderous roar. But happily there was time. The dam was giving way gradually, and had not yet let loose the tremendous volume of death and desolation which it held enclosed within its frail timbers.

The colt, catching the spirit of excitement in the air, flew like the wind, leaving farm after farm behind it, until it reached the village.

"The dam is breaking! Run for your lives! " cried Bonnyboy, with a rousing clarion yell which rose above all other poises; and up and down the valley the dread tidings spread like wildfire. In an instant all was in wildest commotion. Terrified mothers, with babes in their arms, came bursting out of the houses, and little girls, hugging kittens or cages with canary-birds, clung weeping to their skirts; shouting men, shrieking women, crying children, barking dogs, gusty showers sweeping from nowhere down upon the distracted fugitives, and above all the ominous, throbbing, pulsating roar as of a mighty chorus of cataracts. It came nearer and nearer. It filled the great vault of the sky with a rush as of colossal wing-beats. Then there came a deafening creaking and crashing; then a huge brownish-white rolling wall, upon which the moonlight gleamed for an instant, and then the very trump of doom—a writhing, brawling, weltering chaos of cattle, dogs, men, lumber, houses, barns, whirling and struggling upon the destroying flood.

VI.

It was the morning after the disaster. The sun rose red and threatening, circled with a ring of fiery mist. People encamped upon the hill-side greeted each other as on the morn of resurrection. For many were found among the living who were being mourned as dead. Mothers hugged their children with tearful joy, thanking God that they had been spared; and husbands who had heard through the night the agonized cries of their drowning wives, finding them at dawn safe and sound, felt as if they had recovered them from the very gates of death. When all were counted, it was ascertained that but very few of the villagers had been overtaken by the flood. The timely warning had enabled all to save themselves, except some who in their eagerness to rescue their goods had lingered too long. Impoverished most of them were by the loss of their houses and cattle. The calamity was indeed overwhelming. But when they considered how much greater the disaster would have been if the flood had come upon them unheralded, they felt that they had cause for gratitude in the midst of their sorrow. And who was it that brought the tidings that snatched them from the jaws of death? Well, nobody knew. He rode too fast. And each was too much startled by the message to take note of the messenger. But who could he possibly have been? An angel from Heaven, perhaps sent by God in

His mercy. That was indeed more than likely. The belief was at once accepted that the rescuer was an angel from heaven. But just then a lumberman stepped forward who had worked at the mill and said: "It was Bonnyboy, Grim Carpenter's son. I saw him jump on his gray colt. "

Bonnyboy, Grim Carpenter's son. It couldn't be possible. But the lumberman insisted that it was, and they had to believe him, though, of course, it was a disappointment. But where was Bonnyboy? He deserved thanks, surely. And, moreover, that gray colt was a valuable animal. It was to be hoped that it was not drowned.

The water had now subsided, though it yet overflowed the banks; so that trees, bent and splintered by the terrific force of the flood, grew far out in the river. The foul dams had all been swept away, and the tawny torrent ran again with tumultuous rapids in its old channel. Of the mills scarcely a vestige was left except slight cavities in the banks, and a few twisted beams clinging to the rocks where they had stood. The ruins of the village, with jagged chimneys and broken walls, loomed out of a half-inundated meadow, through which erratic currents were sweeping. Here and there lay a dead cow or dog, and in the branches of a maple-tree the carcasses of two sheep were entangled. In this marshy field a stooping figure was seen wading about, as if in search of something. The water broke about his knees, and sometimes reached up to his waist. He stood like one dazed, and stared into the brown swirling torrent. Now he poked something with his boat-hook, now bent down and purled some dead thing out of a copse of shrubbery in which it had been caught. The sun rose higher in the sky, and the red vapors were scattered. But still the old man trudged wearily about, with the stony stare in his eyes, searching for him whom he had lost. One company after another now descended from the hill-sides, and from the high-lying farms which had not been reached by the flood came wagons with provisions and clothes, and men and women eager and anxious to help. They shouted to the old man in the submerged field, and asked what he was looking for. But he only shook his head, as if he did not understand.

"Why, that is old Grim the carpenter, " said someone. "Has anybody seen Bonnyboy? "

But no one had seen Bonnyboy.

"Do you want help? " they shouted to Grim; but they got no answer.

Hour after hour old Grim trudged about in the chilly water searching for his son. Then, about noon, when he had worked his way far down the river, he caught sight of something which made his heart stand still. In a brown pool, in which a half-submerged willow-tree grew, he saw a large grayish shape which resembled a horse. He stretched out the boat-hook and rolled it over. Dumbly, fearlessly, he stood staring into the pool. There lay his son—there lay Bonnyboy stark and dead.

The cold perspiration broke out upon Grim's brow, and his great breast labored. Slowly he stooped down, drew the dead body out of the water, and tenderly laid it across his knees. He stared into the sightless eyes, and murmuring a blessing, closed them. There was a large discolored spot on the forehead, as of a bruise. Grim laid his hand softly upon it, and stroked away the yellow tuft of hair.

"My poor lad, " he said, while the tears coursed down his wrinkled cheeks, "you had a weak head, but your heart, Bonnyboy—your heart was good. "

THE CHILD OF LUCK

I.

A sunny-tempered little fellow was Hans, and his father declared that he had brought luck with him when he came into the world.

"He was such a handsome baby when he was born, " said Inga, his mother; "but you would scarcely believe it now, running about as he does in forest and field, tearing his clothes and scratching his face. "

Now, it was true, as Hans's mother said, that he did often tear his clothes; and as he had an indomitable curiosity, and had to investigate everything that came in his way, it was also no uncommon thing for him to come home with his face stung or scratched.

"Why must you drag that child with you wherever you go, Nils? " the mother complained to Hans's father, when the little boy was brought to her in such a disreputable condition. "Why can't you leave him at home? What other man do you know who carries a six-year-old little fellow about with him in rain and shine, storm and quiet?

"Well, " Nils invariably answered, "I like him and he likes me. He brings me luck. "

This was a standing dispute between Nils and Inga, his wife, and they never came to an agreement. She knew as well as her husband that before little Hans was born there was want and misery in their cottage. But from the hour the child lifted up its tiny voice, announcing its arrival, there had been prosperity and contentment. Their luck had turned, Nils said, and it was the child that had turned it. They had been married for four years, and though they had no one to provide for but themselves, they scarcely managed to keep body and soul together. All sorts of untoward things happened. Now a tree which he was cutting down fell upon Nils and laid him up for a month; now he got water on his knee from a blow he received while rolling logs into the chute; now the pig died which was to have provided them with salt pork for the winter, and the hens took to the bush, and laid their eggs where nobody except the rats and the weasels could find them. But since little Hans had come and put an end to all these disasters, his father had a superstitious feeling that he could not bear to have him away from him. Therefore every morning when he started out for the forest or the river he carried Hans on his shoulder. And the little boy sat there, smiling proudly and waving his hand to his mother, who stood in the door looking longingly after him.

"Hello, little chap! " cried the lumbermen, when they saw him. "Good-morning to you and good luck! "

They always cheered up, however bad the weather was, when they saw little Hans, for nobody could look at his sunny little face without feeling something like a ray of sunlight stealing into his heart. Hans had a smile and a wave of his hand for everybody. He knew all the lumbermen by name, and they knew him.

They sang as they swung the axe or the boat-hook, and the work went merrily when little Hans sat on the top of the log pile and shouted to them. But if by chance he was absent for a day or two they missed him. No songs were heard, but harsh words, and not infrequently quarrels. Now, nobody believed, of course, that little Hans was such a wizard that he could make people feel and behave any better than it was in their nature to do; but sure it was—at least the lumbermen insisted that it was so—there was joy and good-tempered mirth wherever that child went, and life seemed a little sadder and poorer to those who knew him when he was away.

No one will wonder that Nils sometimes boasted of his little son.

He told not once, but a hundred times, as they sat about the camp-fire eating their dinner, that little Hans was a child of luck, and that no misfortune could happen while he was near. Lumbermen are naturally superstitious, and though perhaps at first they may have had their doubts, they gradually came to accept the statement without question. They came to regard it as a kind of right to have little Hans sit on the top of the log pile when they worked, or running along the chute, while the wild-cat strings of logs shot down the steep slide with lightning speed. They were not in the least afraid lest the logs should jump the chute, as they had often done before, killing or maiming the unhappy man that came too near. For was not little Hans's life charmed, so that no harm could befall him?

Now, it happened that Inga, little Hans's mother, came one day to the river to see how he was getting on. Nils was then standing on a raft hooking the floating logs with his boat-hook, while the boy was watching him from the shore, shouting to him, throwing chips into the water, and amusing himself as best he could. It was early in May, and the river was swollen from recent thaws. Below the cataract where the lumbermen worked, the broad, brown current moved slowly along with sluggish whirls and eddies; but the raft was moored by chains to the shore, so that it was in no danger of getting adrift. It was capital fun to see the logs come rushing down the slide, plunging with a tremendous splash into the river, and then bob up like live things after having bumped against the bottom. Little Hans clapped his hands and yelled with delight when a string of three or four came tearing along in that way, and dived, one after the other, headlong into the water.

"Catch that one, papa! " he cried; "that is a good big fellow. He dived like a man, he did. He has washed the dirt off his snout now; that was the reason he took such a big plunge. "

Nils never failed to reach his boat-hook after the log little Hans indicated, for he liked to humor him, and little Hans liked to be humored. He had an idea that he was directing his father's work, and Nils invented all sorts of innocent devices to flatter little Hans's dignity, and make him think himself indispensable. It was of no use, therefore, for poor Inga to beg little Hans to go home with her. He had so much to do, he said, that he couldn't. He even tried to tear himself away from his mother when she took him by the arm and remonstrated with him. And then and there the conviction stole upon Inga that her child did not love her. She was nothing to him compared to what his father was. And was it right for Nils thus to rob her of the boy's affection? Little Hans could scarcely be blamed for loving his father better; for love is largely dependent upon habit, and Nils had been his constant companion since he was a year old. A bitter sense of loneliness and loss overcame the poor wife as she stood on the river-bank pleading with her child, and finding that she annoyed instead of moving him.

"Won't you come home with mamma, little Hans? " she asked, tearfully. "The kitten misses you very much; it has been mewing for you all the morning. "

"No, " said little Hans, thrusting his hands into his pockets, and turning about with a manly stride; "we are going to have the lumber inspector here to-day? and then papa's big raft is going down the river. "

"But this dreadful noise, dear; how can you stand it? And the logs shooting down that slide and making such a racket. And these great piles of lumber, Hans—think, if they should tumble down and kill you! "

"Oh, I'm not afraid, mamma, " cried Hans, proudly; and, to show his fearlessness, he climbed up the log pile, and soon stood on the top of it, waving his cap and shouting.

"Oh, do come down, child—do come down! " begged Inga, anxiously.

She had scarcely uttered the words when she heard a warning shout from the slope above, and had just time to lift her eyes, when she saw a big black object dart past her, strike the log pile, and break with a deafening crash. A long confused rumble of rolling logs followed, terrified voices rent the air, and, above it all, the deep and steady roar of the cataract. She saw, as through a fog, little Hans, serene and smiling as ever, borne down on the top of the rolling lumber, now rising up and skipping from log to log, now clapping his hands and screaming with pleasure, and then suddenly vanishing in the brown writhing river. His laughter was still ringing in her ears; the poor child, he did not realize his danger. The rumbling of falling logs continued with terrifying persistence. Splash! splash! splash! they went, diving by twos, by fours, and by dozens at the very spot where her child had vanished. But where was little Hans? Oh, where was he? It was all so misty, so unreal and confused. She could not tell whether little Hans was among the living or among the dead. But there, all of a sudden, his head popped up in the middle of the river; and there was another head close to his—it was that of his father! And round about them other heads bobbed up; for all the lumbermen who were on the raft had plunged into the water with Nils when they saw that little Hans was in danger. A dozen more were running down the slope as fast as their legs could carry them; and they gave a tremendous cheer when they saw little Hans's face above the water. He looked a trifle pale and shivery, and he gave a funny little snort, so that the water spurted from his nose. He had lost his hat, but he did not seem to be hurt. His little arms clung tightly about his father's neck, while Nils, dodging the bobbing logs, struck out with all his might for the shore. And when he felt firm bottom under his feet, and came stumbling up through the shallow water, looking like a drowned rat, what a welcome he received from the lumbermen! They all wanted to touch little Hans and pat his cheek, just to make sure that it was really he.

"It was wonderful indeed, " they said, "that he ever came up out of that horrible jumble of pitching and diving logs. He is a child of luck, if ever there was one. "

Not one of them thought of the boy's mother, and little Hans himself scarcely thought of her, elated as he was at the welcome he received from the lumbermen. Poor Inga stood dazed, struggling with a horrible feeling, seeing her child passed from one to the other, while she herself claimed no share in him. Somehow the thought stung her. A sudden clearness burst upon her; she rushed forward, with a piercing scream, snatched little Hans from his father's arms, and hugging his wet little shivering form to her breast, fled like a deer through the underbrush.

From that day little Hans was not permitted to go to the river. It was in vain that Nils pleaded and threatened. His wife acted so unreasonably when that question was broached that he saw it was useless to discuss it. She seized little Hans as a tigress might seize her young, and held him tightly clasped, as if daring anybody to take him away from her. Nils knew it would require force to get his son back again, and that he was not ready to employ. But all joy seemed to have gone out of his life since he had lost the daily companionship of little Hans. His work became drudgery; and all the little annoyances of life, which formerly he had brushed away as one brushes a fly from his nose, became burdens and calamities. The raft upon which he had expended so much labor went to pieces during a sudden rise of the river the night after little Hans's adventure, and three days later Thorkel Fossen was killed outright by a string of logs that jumped the chute.

"It isn't the same sort of place since you took little Hans away, " the lumbermen would often say to Nils. "There's no sort of luck in anything. "

Sometimes they taunted him with want of courage, and called him a "night-cap" and a "hen-pecked coon, " all of which made Nils uncomfortable. He made two or three attempts to persuade his wife to change her mind in regard to little Hans, but the last time she got so frightened that she ran out of the house and hid in the cow stable with the boy, crouching in an empty stall, and crying as if her heart would break, when little Hans escaped and betrayed her hiding-place. The boy, in fact, sympathized with his father, and found his confinement at home irksome. The companionship of the cat had no more charm for him; and even the brindled calf, which had caused such an excitement when he first arrived, had become an old story. Little Halls fretted, was mischievous for want of better employment, and gave his mother no end of trouble. He longed for the gay and animated life at the river, and he would have run away if he had not been watched. He could not imagine how the lumbermen could be getting on without him. It seemed to him that all work must come to a stop when he was no longer sitting on the top of the log piles, or standing on the bank throwing chips into the water.

Now, as a matter of fact, they were not getting on very well at the river without little Hans. The luck had deserted them, the lumbermen said; and whatever mishaps they had, they attributed to the absence of little Hans. They came to look with ill-suppressed hostility at Nils, whom they regarded as responsible for their misfortunes. For they could scarcely believe that he was quite in earnest in his desire for the boy's return, otherwise they could not comprehend how his wife could dare to oppose him. The weather was stormy, and the mountain brook which ran along the slide concluded to waste no more labor in carving out a bed for itself in the rock, when it might as well be using the slide which it found ready made. And one fine day it broke into the slide and half filled it, so that the logs, when they were started down the steep incline, sent the water flying, turned somersaults, stood on end, and played no end of dangerous tricks which no one could foresee. Several men were badly hurt by beams shooting like rockets through the air, and old Mads Furubakken was knocked senseless and carried home for dead. Then the lumbermen held a council, and made up their minds to get little Hans by fair means or foul. They thought first of sending a delegation of four or five men that very morning, but finally determined to march up to Nils's cottage in a body and demand the boy. There were twenty of them at the very least, and the tops of their long boat-hooks, which they carried on their shoulders, were seen against the green forest before they were themselves visible.

Nils, who was just out of bed, was sitting on the threshold smoking his pipe and pitching a ball to little Hans, who laughed with delight whenever he caught it. Inga was bustling about inside the house, preparing breakfast, which was to consist of porridge, salt herring, and baked potatoes. It had rained during the night, and the sky was yet overcast, but the sun was struggling to break through the cloud-banks. A couple of thrushes in the alder-bushes about the cottage were rejoicing at the change in the weather, and Nils was listening to their song and to his son's merry prattle, when he caught sight of the twenty lumbermen marching up the hillside. He rose, with some astonishment, and went to meet them. Inga, hearing their voices, came to the door, and seeing the many men, snatched up little Hans, and with a wildly palpitating heart ran into the cottage, bolting the door behind her. She had a vague foreboding that this unusual visit meant something hostile to herself, and she guessed that Nils had been only the spokesman of his comrades in demanding so eagerly the return of the boy to the river. She believed all their talk about his luck to be idle nonsense; but she knew that Nils had unwittingly spread this belief, and that the lumbermen were convinced that little Hans was their good genius, whose presence averted disaster. Distracted with fear and anxiety, she stood pressing her ear against the crack in the door, and sometimes peeping out to see what measures she must take for the child's safety. Would Nils stand by her, or would he desert her? But surely—what was Nils thinking about? He was extending his hand to each of the men, and receiving them kindly.

Next he would be inviting them to come in and take little Hans. She saw one of the men—Stubby Mons by name—step forward, and she plainly heard him say:

"We miss the little chap down at the river, Nils. The luck has been against us since he left. "

"Well, Mons, " Nils answered, "I miss the little chap as much as any of you; perhaps more. But my wife—she's got a sort of crooked notion that the boy won't come home alive if she lets him go to the river. She got a bad scare last time, and it isn't any use arguing with her. "

"But won't you let us talk to her, Nils? " one of the lumbermen proposed. "It is a tangled skein, and I don't pretend to say that I can straighten it out. But two men have been killed and one crippled since the little chap was taken away. And in the three years he was with us no untoward thing happened. Now that speaks for itself, Nils, doesn't it? "

"It does, indeed, " said Nils, with an air of conviction.

"And you'll let us talk to your wife, and see if we can't make her listen to reason, " the man urged.

"You are welcome to talk to her as much as you like, " Nils replied, knocking out his pipe on the heel of his boot; "but I warn you that she's mighty cantankerous. "

He rose slowly, and tried to open the door. It was locked. "Open, Inga, " he said, a trifle impatiently; "there are some men here who want to see you. "

II.

Inga sat crouching on the hearth, hugging little Hans to her bosom. She shook and trembled with fear, let her eyes wander around the walls, and now and then moaned at the thought that now they would take little Hans away from her.

"Why don't you open the door for papa? " asked little Hans, wonderingly.

Ah, he too was against her! All the world was against her! And her husband was in league with her enemies!

"Open, I say! " cried Nils, vehemently. "What do you mean by locking the door when decent people come to call upon us? "

Should she open the door or should she not? Holding little Hans in her arms, she rose hesitatingly, and stretched out her hand toward the bolt. But all of a sudden, in a paroxysm of fear, she withdrew her hand, turned about, and fled with the child through the back door. The alder bushes grew close up to the walls of the cottage, and by stooping a little she managed to remain unobserved. Her greatest difficulty was to keep little Hans from shouting to his father, and she had to put her hand over his mouth to keep him quiet; for the boy, who had heard the voices without, could not understand why he should not be permitted to go out and converse with his friends the lumbermen. The wild eyes and agitated face of his mother distressed him, and the little showers of last night's rain which the trees shook down upon him made him shiver.

"Why do you run so, mamma? " he asked, when she removed her hand from his mouth.

"Because the bad men want to take you away from me, Hans, " she answered, panting.

"Those were not bad men, mamma, " the boy ejaculated. "That was Stubby Mons and Stuttering Peter and Lars Skin-breeches. They don't, want to hurt me. "

He expected that his mamma would be much relieved at receiving this valuable information, and return home without delay. But she still pressed on, flushed and panting, and cast the same anxious glances behind her.

In the meanwhile Nils and his guests had entirely lost their patience. Finding his persuasions of no avail, the former began to thump at the door with the handle of his axe, and receiving no response, he climbed up to the window and looked in. To his amazement there was no one in the room. Thinking that Inga might have gone to the cow-stable, he ran to the rear of the cottage, and called her name. Still no answer.

"Hans, " he cried, "where are you? "

But Hans, too, was as if spirited away. It scarcely occurred to Nils, until he had searched the cow- stable and the house in vain, that his wife had fled from the harmless lumbermen. Then the thought shot through his brain that possibly she was not quite right in her head; that this fixed idea that everybody wanted to take her child away from her had unsettled her reason. Nils grew hot and cold in the same moment as this dreadful apprehension took lodgement in his mind. Might she not, in her confused effort to save little Hans, do him harm? In the blind and feverish terror which possessed her might she not rush into the water, or leap over a precipice? Visions of little Hans drowning, or whirled into the abyss in his mother's arms, crowded his fancy as he walked back to the lumbermen, and told them that neither his wife nor child was anywhere to be found.

"I would ask ye this, lads, " he said, finally: "if you would help me search for them. For Inga—I reckon she is a little touched in the upper story—she has gone off with the boy, and I can't get on without little Hans any more than you can. "

The men understood the situation at a glance, and promised their aid. They had all looked upon Inga as "high-strung" and "queer, " and it did not surprise them to hear that she had been frightened out of her wits at their request for the loan of little Hans. Forming a line, with a space of twenty feet between each man, they began to beat the bush, climbing the steep slope toward the mountains. Inga, pausing for an instant, and peering out between the tree trunks, saw the alder bushes wave as they broke through the underbrush. She knew now that she was pursued. Tired she was, too, and the boy grew heavier for every step that she advanced. And yet if she made him walk, he might run away from her. If he heard his father's voice, he would be certain to answer. Much perplexed, she looked about her for a hiding-place.

For, as the men would be sure to overtake her, her only safety was in hiding. With tottering knees she stumbled along, carrying the heavy child, grabbing hold of the saplings for support, and yet scarcely keeping from falling. The cold perspiration broke from her brow and a strange faintness overcame her.

"You will have to walk, little Hans, " she said, at last. "But if you run away from me, dear, I shall lie down here and die. "

Little Hans promised that he would not run away, and for five minutes they walked up a stony path which looked like the abandoned bed of a brook.

"You hurt my hand, mamma, " whimpered the boy, "you squeeze so hard. "

She would have answered, but just then she heard the voices of the lumbermen scarcely fifty paces away. With a choking sensation and a stitch in her side she pressed on, crying out in spirit for the hills to hide her and the mountains to open their gates and receive her. Suddenly she stood before a rocky wall some eighty or a hundred feet high. She could go no farther. Her strength was utterly exhausted. There was a big boulder lying at the base of the rock, and a spreading juniper half covered it. Knowing that in another minute she would be discovered, she flung herself down behind the boulder, though the juniper needles scratched her face, and pulled little Hans down at her side. But, strange to say, little Hans fell farther than she had calculated, and utterly-vanished from sight. She heard a muffled cry, and reaching her hand in the direction where he had fallen, caught hold of his arm. A strong, wild smell beat against her, and little Hans, as he was pulled out, was enveloped in a most unpleasant odor. But odor or no odor, here was the very hiding-place she had been seeking. A deserted wolf's den, it was, probably—at least she hoped it was deserted; for if it was not, she might be confronted with even uglier customers than the lumbermen. But she had no time for debating the question, for she saw the head of Stubby Mons emerging from the leaves, and immediately behind him came Stuttering Peter, with his long boat-hook. Quick as a flash she slipped into the hole, and dragged Hans after her. The juniper-bush entirely covered the entrance. She could see everyone who approached, without being seen. Unhappily, the boy too caught sight of Stubby Mons, and called him by name. The lumberman stopped and pricked up his ears.

"Did you hear anybody call? " he asked his companion.

"N-n-n-n-aw, I d-d-d-d-didn't, " answered Stuttering Peter. "There b-be lots of qu-qu-qu-qu-eer n-noises in the w-w-w-woods. "

Little Hans heard every word that they spoke, and he would have cried out again, if it hadn't appeared such great fun to be playing hide-and-go-seek with the lumbermen. He had a delicious sense of being well hidden, and had forgotten everything except the zest of the game. Most exciting it became when Stubby Mons drew the juniper-bush aside and peered eagerly behind the boulder. Inga's heart stuck in her throat; she felt sure that in the next instant they would be discovered. And as ill-luck would have it, there was something alive scrambling about her feet and tugging at her skirts. Suddenly she felt a sharp bite, but clinched her teeth, and uttered no sound. When her vision again cleared, the juniper branch had rebounded into its place, and the face of Stubby Mons was gone. She drew a deep breath of relief, but yet did not dare to emerge from the den. For one, two, three tremulous minutes she remained motionless, feeling all the while that uncomfortable sensation of living things about her.

At last she could endure it no longer. Thrusting little Hans before her, she crawled out of the hole, and looked back into the small cavern. As soon as her eyes grew accustomed to the twilight she uttered a cry of amazement, for out from her skirts jumped a little gray furry object, and two frisky little customers of the same sort were darting about among the stones and tree-roots. The truth dawned upon her, and it chilled her to the marrow of her bones. The wolf's den was not deserted. The old folks were only out hunting, and the shouting and commotion of the searching party had probably prevented them from returning in time to look after their family. She seized little Hans by the hand, and once more dragged him away over the rough path. He soon became tired and fretful, and in spite of all her entreaties began to shout lustily for his father. But the men were now so far away that they could not hear him. He complained of hunger; and when presently they came to a blueberry patch, she flung herself down on the heather and allowed him to pick berries. She heard cow-bells and sheep-bells tinkling round about her, and concluded that she could not be far from the saeters, or mountain dairies. That was fortunate, indeed, for she would not have liked to sleep in the woods with wolves and bears prowling about her.

She was just making an effort to rise from the stone upon which she was sitting, when the big, good-natured face of a cow broke through the leaves and stared at her. There was again help in need. She approached the cow, patted it, and calling little Hans, bade him sit down in the heather and open his mouth. He obeyed rather wonderingly, but perceived his mother's intent when she knelt at his side and began to milk into his mouth. It seemed to him that he had never tasted anything so delicious as this fresh rich milk, fragrant with the odor of the woods and the succulent mountain grass. When his hunger was satisfied, he fell again to picking berries, while Inga refreshed herself with milk in the same simple fashion. After having rested a full hour, she felt strong enough to continue her journey; and hearing the loor, or Alpine horn, re-echoing among the mountains, she determined to follow the sound. It was singular what luck attended her in the midst of her misfortune. Perhaps it was, after all, no idle tale that little Hans was a child of luck; and she had done the lumbermen injustice in deriding their faith in him. Perhaps there was some guiding Providence in all that had happened, destined in the end to lead little Hans to fortune and glory. Much encouraged by this thought, she stooped over him and kissed him;

then took his hand and trudged along over logs and stones, through juniper and bramble bushes.

"Mamma, " said little Hans, "where are you going? "

"I am going to the saeter, " she answered; "where you have wanted so often to go. "

"Then why don't you follow the cows? They are going there too. "

Surely that child had a marvellous mind! She smiled down upon him and nodded. By following the cows they arrived in twenty minutes at a neat little log cabin, from which the smoke curled up gayly into the clear air.

The dairy-maids who spent the summer there tending the cattle both fell victims to the charms of little Hans, and offered him and his mother their simple hospitality. They told of the lumbermen who had passed the saeter huts, and inquired for her; but otherwise they respected her silence, and made no attempt to pry into her secrets. The next morning she started, after a refreshing sleep, westward toward the coast, where she hoped in some way to find a passage to America. For if little Hans was really born under a lucky star—which fact she now could scarcely doubt—then America was the place for him. There he might rise to become President, or a judge, or a parson, or something or other; while in Norway he would never be anything but a lumberman like his father. Inga had a well-to-do sister, who was a widow, in the nearest town, and she would borrow enough money from her to pay their passage to New York.

It was early in July when little Hans and his mother arrived in New York. The latter had repented bitterly of her rashness in stealing her child from his father, and under a blind impulse traversing half the globe in a wild-goose chase after fortune. The world was so much bigger than she in her quiet valley had imagined; and, what was worse, it wore such a cold and repellent look, and was so bewildering and noisy. Inga had been very sea-sick during the voyage; and after she stepped ashore from the tug that brought her to Castle Garden, the ground kept heaving and swelling under her feet, and made her dizzy and miserable. She had been very wicked, she was beginning to think, and deserved punishment; and if it had not been for a vague and adventurous faith in the great future that was in store for her son, she would have been content to return home, do penance for her folly, and beg her husband's forgiveness. But, in the first place, she had no money to pay for a return ticket; and, secondly, it would be a great pity to deprive little Hans of the Presidency and all the grandeur that his lucky star might here bring him.

Inga was just contemplating this bright vision of Hans's future, when she found herself passing through a gate, at which a clerk was seated.

"What is your name? " he asked, through an interpreter.

"Inga Olsdatter Pladsen. "

"Age? "

"Twenty-eight a week after Michaelmas. "

"Single or married? "

"Married. "

"Where is your husband? "

"In Norway. "

"Are you divorced from him? "

"Divorced—I! Why, no! Who ever heard of such a thing? "

Inga grew quite indignant at the thought of her being divorced. A dozen other questions were asked, at each of which her embarrassment increased. When, finally, she declared that she had no money, no definite destination, and no relatives or friends in the country, the examination was cut short, and after an hour's delay and a wearisome cross-questioning by different officials, she was put on board the tug, and returned to the steamer in which she had crossed the ocean. Four dreary days passed; then there was a tremendous commotion on deck: blowing of whistles, roaring of steam, playing of bands, bumping of trunks and boxes, and finally the steady pulsation of the engines as the big ship stood out to sea. After nine days of discomfort in the stuffy steerage and thirty-six hours of downright misery while crossing the stormy North Sea,

Inga found herself once more in the land of her birth. Full of humiliation and shame she met her husband at the railroad station, and prepared herself for a deluge of harsh words and reproaches. But instead of that he patted her gently on the head, and clasped little Hans in his arms and kissed him. They said very little to each other as they rode homeward in the cars; but little Hans had a thousand things to tell, and his father was delighted to hear them. In the evening, when they had reached their native valley, and the boy was asleep, Inga plucked up courage and said, "Nils, it is all a mistake about little Hans's luck. "

"Mistake! Why, no, " cried Nils. "What greater luck could he have than to be brought safely home to his father? "

Inga had indeed hoped for more; but she said nothing. Nevertheless, fate still had strange things in store for little Hans. The story of his mother's flight to and return from America was picked up by some enterprising journalist, who made a most touching romance of it. Hundreds of inquiries regarding little Hans poured in upon the pastor and the postmaster; and offers to adopt him, educate him, and I know not what else, were made to his parents. But Nils would hear of no adoption; nor would he consent to any plan that separated him from the boy. When, however, he was given a position as superintendent of a lumber yard in the town, and prosperity began to smile upon him, he sent little Hans to school, and as Hans was a clever boy, he made the most of his opportunities.

And now little Hans is indeed a very big Hans, but a child of luck he is yet; for I saw him referred to the other day in the newspapers as one of the greatest lumber dealers, and one of the noblest, most generous, and public-spirited men in Norway.

THE BEAR THAT HAD A BANK ACCOUNT

I.

You may not believe it, but the bear I am going to tell you about really had a bank account! He lived in the woods, as most bears do; but he had a reputation which extended over all Norway and more than half of England. Earls and baronets came every summer, with repeating-rifles of the latest patent, and plaids and field-glasses and portable cooking-stoves, intent upon killing him. But Mr. Bruin, whose only weapons were a pair of paws and a pair of jaws, both uncommonly good of their kind, though not patented, always managed to get away unscathed; and that was sometimes more than the earls and the baronets did.

One summer the Crown Prince of Germany came to Norway. He also heard of the famous bear that no one could kill, and made up his mind that he was the man to kill it. He trudged for two days through bogs, and climbed through glens and ravines, before he came on the scent of a bear, and a bear's scent, you may know, is strong, and quite unmistakable. Finally he discovered some tracks in the moss, like those of a barefooted man, or, I should rather say, perhaps, a man-footed bear. The Prince was just turning the corner of a projecting rock, when he saw a huge, shaggy beast standing on its hind legs, examining in a leisurely manner the inside of a hollow tree, while a swarm of bees were buzzing about its ears. It was just hauling out a handful of honey, and was smiling with a grewsome mirth, when His Royal Highness sent it a bullet right in the breast, where its heart must have been, if it had one. But, instead of falling down flat, as it ought to have done, out of deference to the Prince, it coolly turned its back, and gave its assailant a disgusted nod over its shoulder as it trudged away through the underbrush. The attendants ranged through the woods and beat the bushes in all directions, but Mr. Bruin was no more to be seen that afternoon. It was as if he had sunk into the earth; not a trace of him was to be found by either dogs or men.

From that time forth the rumor spread abroad that this Gausdale Bruin (for that was the name by which he became known) was enchanted. It was said that he shook off bullets as a duck does water; that he had the evil eye, and could bring misfortune to whomsoever he looked upon. The peasants dreaded to meet him, and ceased to hunt him. His size was described as something enormous, his teeth, his claws, and his eyes as being diabolical beyond human conception. In the meanwhile Mr. Bruin had it all his own way in the mountains, killed a young bull or a fat heifer for his dinner every day or two, chased in pure sport a herd of sheep over a precipice; and as for Lars Moe's bay mare Stella, he nearly finished her, leaving his claw-marks on her flank in a way that spoiled her beauty forever.

Now Lars Moe himself was too old to hunt; and his nephew was—well, he was not old enough. There was, in fact, no one in the valley who was of the right age to hunt this Gausdale Bruin. It was of no use that Lars Moe egged on the young lads to try their luck, shaming them, or offering them rewards, according as his mood might happen to be. He was the wealthiest man in the valley, and his mare Stella had been the apple of his eye. He felt it as a personal insult that the bear should have dared to molest what belonged to him, especially the most precious of all his possessions. It cut him to the heart to see the poor wounded beauty, with those cruel scratches on her thigh, and one stiff, aching leg done up in oil and cotton. When he opened the stable-door, and was greeted by Stella's low, friendly neighing, or when she limped forward in her box-stall and put her small, clean-shaped head on his shoulder, then Lars Moe's heart swelled until it seemed on the point of breaking. And so it came to pass that he added a codicil to his will, setting aside five hundred dollars of his estate as a reward to the man who, within six years, should kill the Gausdale Bruin.

Soon after that, Lars Moe died, as some said, from grief and chagrin; though the physician affirmed that it was of rheumatism of the heart. At any rate, the codicil relating to the enchanted bear was duly read before the church door, and pasted, among other legal notices, in the vestibules of the judge's and the sheriff's offices. When the executors had settled up the estate, the question arose in whose name or to whose credit should be deposited the money which was to be set aside for the benefit of the bear-slayer. No one knew who would kill the bear, or if any one would kill it. It was a puzzling question.

"Why, deposit it to the credit of the bear, " said a jocose executor; "then, in the absence of other heirs, his slayer will inherit it. That is good old Norwegian practice, though I don't know whether it has ever been the law. "

"All right, " said the other executors, "so long as it is understood who is to have the money, it does not matter. "

And so an amount equal to $500 was deposited in the county bank to the credit of the Gausdale Bruin. Sir Barry Worthington, Bart., who came abroad the following summer for the shooting, heard the story, and thought it a good one. So, after having vainly tried to earn the prize himself, he added another $500 to the deposit, with the stipulation that he was to have the skin.

But his rival for parliamentary honors, Robert Stapleton, Esq., the great iron-master, who had come to Norway chiefly to outshine Sir Barry, determined that he was to have the skin of that famous bear, if any one was to have it, and that, at all events, Sir Barry should not have it. So Mr. Stapleton added $750 to the bear's bank account, with the stipulation that the skin should come to him.

Mr. Bruin, in the meanwhile, as if to resent this unseemly contention about his pelt, made worse havoc among the herds than ever, and compelled several peasants to move their dairies to other parts of the mountains, where the pastures were poorer, but where they would be free from his depredations. If the $1,750 in the bank had been meant as a bribe or a stipend for good behavior, such as was formerly paid to Italian brigands, it certainly could not have been more demoralizing in its effect; for all agreed that, since Lars Moe's death, Bruin misbehaved worse than ever.

II.

There was an odd clause in Lars Moe's will besides the codicil relating to the bear. It read:

"I hereby give and bequeath to my daughter Unna, or, in case of her decease, to her oldest living issue, my bay mare Stella, as a token that I have forgiven her the sorrow she caused me by her marriage. "

It seemed incredible that Lars Moe should wish to play a practical joke (and a bad one at that) on his only child, his daughter Unna, because she had displeased him by her marriage. Yet that was the common opinion in the valley when this singular clause became known. Unna had married Thorkel Tomlevold, a poor tenant's son, and had refused her cousin, the great lumber-dealer, Morten Janson, whom her father had selected for a son-in-law.

She dwelt now in a tenant's cottage, northward in the parish; and her husband, who was a sturdy and fine-looking fellow, eked out a living by hunting and fishing. But they surely had no accommodations for a broken-down, wounded, trotting mare, which could not even draw a plough. It is true Unna, in the days of her girlhood, had been very fond of the mare, and it is only charitable to suppose that the clause, which was in the body of the will, was written while Stella was in her prime, and before she had suffered at the paws of the Gausdale Bruin. But even granting that, one could scarcely help suspecting malice aforethought in the curious provision. To Unna the gift was meant to say, as plainly as possible, "There, you see what you have lost by disobeying your father! If you had married according to his wishes, you would have been able to accept the gift, while now you are obliged to decline it like a beggar."

But if it was Lars Moe's intention to convey such a message to his daughter, he failed to take into account his daughter's spirit. She appeared plainly but decently dressed at the reading of the will, and carried her head not a whit less haughtily than was her wont in her maiden days. She exhibited no chagrin when she found that Janson was her father's heir and that she was disinherited. She even listened with perfect composure to the reading of the clause which bequeathed to her the broken-down mare.

It at once became a matter of pride with her to accept her girlhood's favorite, and accept it she did! And having borrowed a side-saddle, she rode home, apparently quite contented. A little shed, or lean-to, was built in the rear of the house, and Stella became a member of Thorkel Tomlevold's family. Odd as it may seem, the fortunes of the family took a turn for the better from the day she arrived; Thorkel rarely came home without big game, and in his traps he caught more than any three other men in all the parish.

"The mare has brought us luck, " he said to his wife. "If she can't plough, she can at all events pull the sleigh to church; and you have as good a right as any one to put on airs, if you choose. "

"Yes, she has brought us blessing, " replied Unna, quietly; "and we are going to keep her till she dies of old age. "

To the children Stella became a pet, as much as if she had been a dog or a cat. The little boy Lars climbed all over her, and kissed her regularly good-morning when she put her handsome head in

141

through the kitchen-door to get her lump of sugar. She was as gentle as a lamb and as intelligent as a dog. Her great brown eyes, with their soft, liquid look, spoke as plainly as words could speak, expressing pleasure when she was patted; and the low neighing with which she greeted the little boy, when she heard his footsteps in the door, was to him like the voice of a friend.

He grew to love this handsome and noble animal as he had loved nothing on earth except his father and mother.

As a matter of course he heard a hundred times the story of Stella's adventure with the terrible Gausdale bear. It was a story that never lost its interest, that seemed to grow more exciting the oftener it was told. The deep scars of the bear's claws in Stella's thigh were curiously examined, and each time gave rise to new questions. The mare became quite a heroic character, and the suggestion was frequently discussed between Lars and his little sister Marit, whether Stella might not be an enchanted princess who was waiting for some one to cut off her head, so that she might show herself in her glory. Marit thought the experiment well worth trying, but Lars had his doubts, and was unwilling to take the risk; yet if she brought luck, as his mother said, then she certainly must be something more than an ordinary horse.

Stella had dragged little Lars out of the river when he fell overboard from the pier; and that, too, showed more sense than he had ever known a horse to have.

There could be no doubt in his mind that Stella was an enchanted princess. And instantly the thought occurred to him that the dreadful enchanted bear with the evil eye was the sorcerer, and that, when he was killed, Stella would resume her human guise. It soon became clear to him that he was the boy to accomplish this heroic deed; and it was equally plain to him that he must keep his purpose secret from all except Marit, as his mother would surely discourage him from engaging in so perilous an enterprise. First of all, he had to learn how to shoot; and his father, who was the best shot in the valley, was very willing to teach him. It seemed quite natural to Thorkel that a hunter's son should take readily to the rifle; and it gave him great satisfaction to see how true his boy's aim was, and how steady his hand.

"Father, " said Lars one day, "you shoot so well, why haven't you ever tried to kill the Gausdale Bruin that hurt Stella so badly? "

"Hush, child! you don't know what you are talking about, " answered his father; "no leaden bullet will harm that wicked beast. "

"Why not? "

"I don't like to talk about it—but it is well known that he is enchanted. "

"But will he then live for ever? Is there no sort of bullet that will kill him? " asked the boy.

"I don't know. I don't want to have anything to do with witchcraft, " said Thorkel.

The word "witchcraft" set the boy to thinking, and he suddenly remembered that he had been warned not to speak to an old woman named Martha Pladsen, because she was a witch. Now, she was probably the very one who could tell him what he wanted to know. Her cottage lay close up under the mountain-side, about two miles from his home. He did not deliberate long before going to seek this mysterious person, about whom the most remarkable stories were told in the valley. To his astonishment, she received him kindly, gave him a cup of coffee with rock candy, and declared that she had long expected him. The bullet which was to slay the enchanted bear had long been in her possession; and she would give it to him if he would promise to give her the beast's heart.

He did not have to be asked twice for that; and off he started gayly with his prize in his pocket. It was rather an odd-looking bullet, made of silver, marked with a cross on one side and with a lot of queer illegible figures on the other. It seemed to burn in his pocket, so anxious was he to start out at once to release the beloved Stella from the cruel enchantment. But Martha had said that the bear could only be killed when the moon was full; and until the moon was full he accordingly had to bridle his impatience.

III.

It was a bright morning in January, and, as it happened, Lars's fourteenth birthday. To his great delight, his mother had gone down to the judge's to sell some ptarmigans, and his father had gone to fell some timber up in the glen. Accordingly he could secure the rifle without being observed. He took an affectionate good-by of Stella, who rubbed her soft nose against his own, playfully pulled at his coat-collar, and blew her sweet, warm breath into his face. Lars was a simple-hearted boy, in spite of his age, and quite a child at heart. He had lived so secluded from all society, and breathed so long the atmosphere of fairy tales, that he could see nothing at all absurd in what he was about to undertake. The youngest son in the story-book always did just that sort of thing, and everybody praised and admired him for it. Lars meant, for once, to put the story-book hero into the shade. He engaged little Marit to watch over Stella while he was gone, and under no circumstances to betray him—all of which Marit solemnly promised.

With his rifle on his shoulder and his skees on his feet, Lars glided slowly along over the glittering surface of the snow, for the mountain was steep, and he had to zigzag in long lines before he reached the upper heights, where the bear was said to have his haunts. The place where Bruin had his winter den had once been pointed out to him, and he remembered yet how pale his father was, when he found that he had strayed by chance into so dangerous a neighborhood. Lars's heart, too, beat rather uneasily as he saw the two heaps of stones, called "The Parson" and "The Deacon, " and the two huge fir-trees which marked the dreaded spot. It had been customary from immemorial time for each person who passed along the road to throw a large stone on the Parson's heap, and a small one on the Deacon's; but since the Gausdale Bruin had gone into winter quarters there, the stone heaps had ceased to grow.

Under the great knotted roots of the fir-trees there was a hole, which was more than half-covered with snow; and it was noticeable that there was not a track of bird or beast to be seen anywhere around it. Lars, who on the way had been buoyed up by the sense of his heroism, began now to feel strangely uncomfortable. It was so awfully hushed and still round about him; not the scream of a bird —not even the falling of a broken bough was to be heard. The pines stood in lines and in clumps, solemn, like a funeral procession, shrouded in sepulchral white. Even if a crow had cawed it would have been a relief to the frightened boy—for it must be confessed that he was a trifle frightened—if only a little shower of snow had fallen upon his head from the heavily laden branches, he would have been grateful for it, for it would have broken the spell of this oppressive silence.

There could be no doubt of it; inside, under those tree-roots slept Stella's foe—the dreaded enchanted beast who had put the boldest of hunters to flight, and set lords and baronets by the ears for the privilege of possessing his skin. Lars became suddenly aware that it was a foolhardy thing he had undertaken, and that he had better betake himself home. But then, again, had not Witch-Martha said that she had been waiting for him; that he was destined by fate to accomplish this deed, just as the youngest son had been in the story-book. Yes, to be sure, she had said that; and it was a comforting thought.

Accordingly, having again examined his rifle, which he had carefully loaded with the silver bullet before leaving home, he started boldly forward, climbed up on the little hillock between the two trees, and began to pound it lustily with the butt-end of his gun. He listened for a moment tremulously, and heard distinctly long, heavy sighs from within.

His heart stood still. The bear was awake! Soon he would have to face it! A minute more elapsed; Lars's heart shot up into his throat. He leaped down, placed himself in front of the entrance to the den, and cocked his rifle. Three long minutes passed. Bruin had evidently gone to sleep again. Wild with excitement, the boy rushed forward and drove his skee-staff straight into the den with all his might. A sullen growl was heard, like a deep and menacing thunder. There could be no doubt that now the monster would take him to task for his impertinence.

Again the boy seized his rifle; and his nerves, though tense as stretched bow-strings, seemed suddenly calm and steady. He lifted the rifle to his cheek, and resolved not to shoot until he had a clear aim at heart or brain. Bruin, though Lars could hear him rummaging within, was in no hurry to come out, But he sighed and growled uproariously, and presently showed a terrible, long-clawed paw, which he thrust out through his door and then again withdrew. But apparently it took him a long while to get his mind clear as to the cause of the disturbance; for fully five minutes had elapsed when suddenly a big tuft of moss was tossed out upon the snow, followed by a cloud of dust and an angry creaking of the tree-roots.

Great masses of snow were shaken from the swaying tops of the firs, and fell with light thuds upon the ground. In the face of this unexpected shower, which entirely hid the entrance to the den, Lars was obliged to fall back a dozen paces; but, as the glittering drizzle cleared away, he saw an enormous brown beast standing upon its hind legs, with widely distended jaws. He was conscious of no fear, but of a curious numbness in his limbs, and strange noises, as of warning shouts and cries, filling his ears.

Fortunately, the great glare of the sun-smitten snow dazzled Bruin; he advanced slowly, roaring savagely, but staring rather blindly before him out of his small, evil-looking eyes. Suddenly, when he was but a few yards distant, he raised his great paw, as if to rub away the cobwebs that obscured his sight.

It was the moment for which the boy had waited. Now he had a clear aim! Quickly he pulled the trigger; the shot reverberated from mountain to mountain, and in the same instant the huge brown bulk rolled in the snow, gave a gasp, and was dead! The spell was broken! The silver bullet had pierced his heart. There was a curious unreality about the whole thing to Lars. He scarcely knew whether he was really himself or the hero of the fairy-tale.

All that was left for him to do now was to go home and marry Stella, the delivered princess.

The noises about him seemed to come nearer and nearer; and now they sounded like human voices. He looked about him, and to his amazement saw his father and Marit, followed by two wood-cutters, who, with raised axes, were running toward him. Then he did not know exactly what happened; but he felt himself lifted up by two strong arms, and tears fell hot and fast upon his face.

"My boy! my boy! " said the voice in his ears, "I expected to find you dead. "

"No, but the bear is dead, " said Lars, innocently.

"I didn't mean to tell on you, Lars, " cried Marit, "but I was so afraid, and then I had to. "

The rumor soon filled the whole valley that the great Gausdale Bruin was dead, and that the boy Lars Tomlevold had killed him. It is needless to say that Lars Tomlevold became the parish hero from that day. He did not dare to confess in the presence of all this praise and wonder that at heart he was bitterly disappointed; for when he came home, throbbing with wild expectancy, there stood Stella before the kitchen door, munching a piece of bread; and when she hailed him with a low whinny, he burst into tears. But he dared not tell any one why he was weeping.

This story might have ended here, but it has a little sequel. The $1,750 which Bruin had to his credit in the bank had increased to $2,290; and it was all paid to Lars. A few years later, Martin Janson, who had inherited the estate of Moe from old Lars, failed in consequence of his daring forest speculations, and young Lars was enabled to buy the farm at auction at less than half its value. Thus he had the happiness to bring his mother back to the place of her birth, of which she had been wrongfully deprived; and Stella, who was now twenty-one years old, occupied once more her handsome box-stall, as in the days of her glory. And although she never proved to be a princess, she was treated as if she were one, during the few years that remained to her.